Violencia!

ALSO BY BRUCE JAY FRIEDMAN

Novels
A Father's Kisses
The Current Climate
Tokyo Woes
About Harry Towns
The Dick
A Mother's Kisses
Stern

Short Story Collections
Let's Hear It for a Beautiful Guy
Black Angels
Far from the City of Class
Black Humor: Anthology
The Collected Short Fiction of Bruce Jay Friedman

Plays
Scuba Duba
Steambath
Have You Spoken to Any Jews Lately?

Nonfiction
Even the Rhinos Were Nymphos
The Lonely Guy and The Slightly Older Guy

Violencia!

A MUSICAL NOVEL

Bruce Jay Friedman

Grove Press
New York

Published simultaneously in Canada
Printed in the United States of America

FIRST EDITION

Library of Congress Cataloging-in-Publication Data
Friedman, Bruce Jay, 1930–
    Violencia! : a musical novel / by Bruce Jay Friedman.
      p. cm.
    ISBN 0-8021-3875-6
    1. Theatrical producers and directors—Fiction.   2. Broadway (New York,
N.Y.)—Fiction.   3. Musicals—Fiction.   4. Theater—Fiction.   I. Title.
PS3556.R5 V65 2002
    813'.54—dc21   2001040512

DESIGN BY LAURA HAMMOND HOUGH

Grove Press
841 Broadway
New York, NY 10003

01 02 03 04 10 9 8 7 6 5 4 3 2 1

For the invincible Swiss pikemen of Marignano, defeated by Francois I, 1515

Violencia!

Act One

Scene I

Closing in on age forty and rattled a bit by a recent divorce, Paul Gurney decided to quit his job and try for a completely new start in life. He was a tall, slightly undernourished fellow with no particularly distinguishing characteristics except for a constant look of perplexity on his face, even as he slept. Or so he had been told. For years, he had been attached to a New York homicide bureau as a civilian clerk, getting out a lively monthly newsletter for the dicks called *The Homicider*.

Gurney had no particular idea of where he was headed, but he wasn't especially concerned about it. He had already gotten one offer—to serve as a guide for a two-state dam project out west, taking groups on underground tours and regaling them with anecdotes about the dam's construction and the difficulties faced by early laborers. But he was not convinced he wanted to go in that direction. Detective Turner, his boss in Homicide, had become reliant on Gurney and was not anxious to lose him. He told Gurney he felt it was a mistake for him to leave and tried to dissuade him.

"You are at least a year away," he warned his assistant.

But Gurney stuck to his guns and said he had to try something else in life, even if it was nothing spectacular. Though not an actual favorite, Gurney had been well-liked by the dicks. In the seven years since he had taken over its reins, *The Homicider* had gotten to be quite a respected publication around the Bureau. "My Favorite Collar," written each month by a different dick, was a popular feature. There was a hefty inventory of submissions that were targeted for future issues. The same was true of "Slab Happy," a roundup of amusing overheards at the morgue, written by the assistant coroner, who aspired to become a television gag writer. Gurney's own personal advice column,—"Ask Gurney," was a particular favorite at the Bureau, though the wife of one dick did hold Gurney accountable for her husband's early demise. The columnist had recommended mountain-climbing as a leisure activity for overly stressed homiciders. Shortly afterward, the woman's nearsighted spouse had plunged to his death from a treacherous peak in upstate New York.

But apart from the one episode, Gurney's record as an advice-giver was difficult to question.

Once Detective Turner saw that Gurney was determined to leave, he not only gave him his blessings, but arranged for the Bureau to give him a send-off party.

It was a lively affair. Several of the dicks, who were no great shakes at speaking in public, rose to their feet and gave stumbling testimonials to their colleague.

Gurney, not much of a speaker himself, kept his remarks short and sweet.

"I've made many friends in my eleven years here," he said, "and I'm glad I did."

As he sat down, and the dicks realized they had heard his entire speech, a collective groan could be heard throughout the rented hall. It was the first time Gurney had ever let them down.

Picking up the sentiment of the group, a tall vice dick named Centro asked: "Is that it?"

"That's the long and short of it," Gurney said.

As editor of *The Homicider,* he had been expected to be much more voluble and entertaining. Gurney, once he was seated, did think of several surefire manslaughter jokes, but it seemed embarrassing to ask for the floor again, and so he said no more. When the last portion of baked Alaska had been consumed by the dicks, and the banquet was winding down, he gathered up his farewell gifts, chief among them a dozen drink-holders that were shaped like handcuffs. Gurney then stuffed a few printed programs into his jacket pockets and said goodbye to the assembled detectives. He turned his back, much more easily than he'd expected, on eleven years of homicide.

After his divorce, Gurney had sublet a small apartment in the Village from a young one-armed Irish woman who worked as a civilian assistant in Armed Robbery. The woman appeared to like him, which accounted for her granting Gurney an exceptionally good deal on the rent. Twelve years of married life had at first made the prospect of living alone a little frightening, but he found he enjoyed the simplicity of it—cooking breakfast for himself, keeping the place tidy—and liked taking strolls through the neighborhood. It was a fascinating one, with twisty and mysterious side streets, a surprising number of them specializing in antique music boxes. He hadn't realized there was that great a demand for such a specialized item, and felt a need to stop in and buy one, if for no other reason than to help one of the stores along. Gurney enjoyed looking in the windows of all the shops, even the ones that sold only dresses. He felt sorry for most of them—lonely, defeated little out-of-the-way establishments—and couldn't see how the owners were able to make a go of it, or why they even bothered to keep them open. Just a place to go every day, he guessed.

And what did it say about Gurney that he felt sorrier for stores than he did for people?

It was not a bad time for him at all. At first he felt his serene life was much too good to continue, and that each day was a stolen one; but after a while, he began to think, *Why not*. He had some money saved, his rent was low, and he felt capable of carrying off this cool, pleasant existence for at least a couple of months.

Evenings, Gurney dropped into a fashionable bar and restaurant called Bombola's. It was run by a bluff and hearty-looking man who had been disbarred as an attorney for throwing a client through a window, then spent the next five years trying to get reinstated. When he had finally pulled it off, he announced, perversely, that he had decided to go into the restaurant business.

Gurney had first come across Bombola's when he had been with the Bureau. Prominent men and well-turned-out women were the main clientele. On his early visits, he had felt awkward and out of place in his wide, flowing detective-style pants. But now that he had resigned from the Bureau, he was more at ease about appearing in the plush and cozy little nightspot. Gurney was an outer-rim man, never quite getting a seat at a choice table; on the other hand, Bombola himself, on occasion, would nod in his direction. The bartenders knew him by name, although they tended, annoyingly, to call him "Gurns."

One Friday night, Gurney, seated at the bar, with a soft, comfortable buzz on, and not paying any particular attention to his surroundings, saw a small, slender, sandy-haired man with a neatly trimmed goatee being ushered along to a favored inner-rim table. The woman with the fellow, even by Bombola's standards, was especially attractive. Tall and blonde, she had a quiet air of money and good schools about her, along with a look of mischievous invitation. There was a small gap between her front teeth which did not reduce her appeal. In his current condition, Gurney noticed and admired women but did not particularly lust after them. In some curious way, he was pleased with himself for having arrived at this state. In a move reserved for a select few, Bombola himself took the couple's drink order but did not linger for the traditional embrace. To Gurney's surprise, the man got up from his table, walked to the bar, and asked if he would care to join him.

"If you're sure I'm not intruding," Gurney said. He'd never sat at one of the coveted inner-rim tables.

"Don't be ridiculous," said the man. " We'd love it."

Once they were seated, the fellow introduced himself as Norman Welles, his companion as Tippy Turnbull.

"I'm a composer, Paul, "he said," and I've been a fan of *The Homicider* for quite some time. Not only do I think it's brilliant, but I'm convinced it would make the basis of a terrific Broadway musical comedy. I've gone down the list of possible adapters and come to a conclusion: There's only one person in the world who can possibly write the libretto and bring the material to life on the stage.

"His name," he said, pausing for effect, as if he were delivering an award, "is Paul Gurney."

It was news to Gurney that someone outside of the Bureau was even aware of his publication. And Welles' proposal took him completely by surprise.

Once he had gotten his bearings, Gurney said: "It's nice of you to think of me, Mr. Welles, but I just don't see how I fit into the picture as a librettist. I did write a couple of sketches years back at the community college, but apart from that I have absolutely no experience in the field.

"Plus," he continued, "I've recently gotten divorced, and would just as soon not make any violent swerves in life."

"Then you won't do it," said Welles. "Is that what you're saying?"

"I guess so," said Gurney.

"I knew he wouldn't," Welles said to his lovely companion, with some bitterness in his voice. "He'll suck you in, make you think you've got him, and then pull out."

Gurney thought the man was being surprisingly childish about his position.

"I didn't suck you in," he said. "Besides, you're probably well-fixed. I'm not, and I've got to make sure that what I go into has some kind of payoff. How much money can you make on one of these?"

"Millions, if it works," said Welles. "About thirty-five dollars if it doesn't."

"Then there you are," said Gurney.

"What did I tell you, Tippy," said Welles, erupting once again. "And do you know *why* this is happening?" he asked. "Simple. It's because I want it so much."

With that, he got up from the table and walked toward the door, his friend following along, but not before she'd smiled apologetically at Gurney.

When the couple had left, Bombola sat down beside Gurney for the first time since the ex-dick had become a regular at the restaurant.

"Let me tell you a little bit more about Norman Welles," he said. "He's never actually done a Broadway musical, but years ago he composed the music for a string of tent shows that toured the country and made a lot of money. The shows were pure schlock, but surprisingly, a few of the songs became hits."

Bombola hummed a few, accompanying himself with jolly Vegas-style finger clicks. Though he was far from a buff, Gurney recognized at least one melody.

"Welles hasn't been heard from in recent years," said the restaurateur, "but the guy is loaded. Does he want to work with you?"

"Yes," said Gurney, still enjoying the fact that Bombola was actually sitting at his table. "But I don't think I'll do it. My idea is to coast along for a while. You probably know that I've just gotten divorced."

"Actually, I didn't know that," said Bombola. "But don't coast too long."

Gurney thanked him for the advice, then stretched out a bit and took in the view from the preferential table.

"I'm starved," he said. "Maybe I'll sit right here and try the liver and onions."

"Good call," said the owner. "But try it at the bar. I need the table."

The next week Welles phoned Gurney at his apartment and said that he would like to have lunch with him and a famous director named Clement Hartog who had become interested in the *Homicider* concept. Gurney did not like getting calls at home and found it irritating that the composer had gotten his unlisted number with such apparent ease. The only other calls he had received were for the one-armed Irish woman who had sublet the apartment to him. They were late-night ones from heavily accented men he assumed were her lovers. Gurney was a little short with Welles, but he had heard of Hartog, and thought it might be enjoyable to meet him.

The three had lunch the next day at a midtown restaurant favored by theatre people. Although Gurney did not do so intentionally, he arrived a bit late and was somewhat embarrassed about it. Welles received him warmly, but Clement Hartog seemed annoyed and did not meet his eyes, wheeling about instead to greet several famed actors seated at other tables. He was a watery-eyed man with a head of unruly gray hair and a magnificent profile. When one of the actors approached to shake his hand, Hartog began to do amputee imitations, making his arms disappear in his jacket as though they had been shot off and then dropping to his knees in what appeared to be a takeoff on Toulouse-Lautrec. After ten minutes or so, he seemed to weary of being cool to Gurney. Turning to the ex-dick, his eyes tearing up with sincerity, he said that he had decided to pass on several major projects because his heart wasn't really in them.

"Just once," he said, "I'd like to do a show I really care about. And by God, this material has all the earmarks of being that show. Violence. It's all around us. It's in the air we breathe, and as far as I'm concerned it's the only subject worth dealing with. I love Norman's music and I think his songs can bring it to life."

Gurney was quite flattered at having a man of Hartog's stature present himself in such an honest and naked way. It occurred to him that all of the really great ones were probably that way—secure enough in their abilities to be completely open-faced and candid.

"I'll work with you on it, Paul," said Hartog. "Right by your side, and I've never done that before with a librettist. I think that if we start in a week or so we can have it ready for the fall season. I'd like to call the show *Violencia,* unless one of you fellows has a better idea."

"I love it," said Welles.

"Sounds good to me," said Gurney.

Sitting in the legendary theatrical restaurant, being pursued with such earnestness by Welles and the celebrated director, Gurney, in spite of himself, felt a certain thrumming of excitement. Still, he thought it only fair to tell Hartog about his divorce and his plan to be cautious about taking on any bold new ventures.

"Jesus," said Hartog, "I can imagine how rough that must be. My heart goes out to you. But perhaps this will take your mind off it."

"Well, my mind really is off it," said Gurney.

But as he said this, he felt powerfully drawn toward Hartog and knew he would enjoy discussing his personal problems with the director, who must have been a good fifteen years his senior, and seemed awfully easy to be with.

"Can I have around a week to think it over?"

"You've got it," said Hartog, getting to his feet and shaking Gurney's hand. "And I do hope you'll decide to come in with us."

"Any young puss in the show?" Gurney asked, then whirled around swiftly as if to glare at the individual who had asked the self-conscious question. The coarse phrasing was a carryover from his years at the Bureau.

Hartog smiled weakly and tolerantly.

"Only kidding, " said Gurney, as if to a parent.

But as soon as Hartog had said good-bye and left the restaurant, Welles said: "Don't worry, once we get out of town, there'll be more puss than you can handle."

"Frankly, I don't know if I'll be doing the show," said Gurney, "but that man is certainly impressive."

"We're damned lucky to get him," said Welles. "Not only that, but we kill two birds with one stone. We get Essie Hartog in the lead role. Terrific little actress."

"His wife?"

"His mother," said Welles, calling for the check.

At first Gurney was shocked that Clement Hartog would agree—and even *arrange*—to have his own mother play the lead in a major musical under his direction. It seemed a cynical plan, and Gurney thought he understood the reason for the great director's interest in what had to be considered a strange and flimsy project—at least in this early stage: Obviously, it was the only way for Hartog to get work for his actress mother. But Gurney could not rid himself of the picture of the graying, world-renowned figure, leaning across the table toward him, eyes brimming with sincerity, and expressing with deep conviction what almost certainly had to be honest feelings for *Violencia*. Perhaps Gurney was being too hard on the man.

After mulling over the project for several days, he called John Gable, an ex-newspaperman who had taken over *The Homicider* when Gurney had left. As it turned out, it was Gable, a showbiz buff, who had passed along copies of *The Homicider* to Norman Welles—clearing up that mystery. Gable said that Essie Hartog was indeed a fine actress, although most of her starring roles had been on the Vienna stage some thirty years back. More recently, she had appeared briefly in a highly praised Noh play in Greenwich Village.

"She's good, all right," said Gable, a man not given to passing out compliments lightly, "and there's one thing handy about having her involved."

"What's that?"

"As I recall, she can play either male or female roles."

Gurney kept savoring the news that Essie Hartog was regarded as a brilliant actress. He had been terribly impressed by Clement Hartog; it helped him to know that the director's mother had a reputation of her own and was not just riding along on her famous son's coattails. Gurney, indeed, was quite interested in the project now; a part of him wanted to contact Welles and Hartog immediately, so that they could all get going without delay. What if they took his hesitation to be a lack of interest and decided to pursue another librettist, one with a few shows under his belt? But it had always been difficult for Gurney to go directly after goals he wanted to achieve. He often took the opposite course.

In this case, he decided not to act until the week was up. For all of its appeal, the project loomed as a long and difficult one; as a result, Gurney had the feeling he might not get to do some of the modest, newly divorced things he had begun to enjoy so much. So he did them for the rest of the week. He bought treats like mangoes and Swiss chocolate bars and ate little gourmet meals by himself in the apartment, at all hours, as many as five small ones a day. On Saturday, he had a maid come in; late in the day, he returned to the flat, took off his clothes, lay down on the bed, and took pleasure in the neatness and simplicity of the place. He enjoyed everything that week: making a couple of pieces of toast, the radio, the fresh December air, and mostly just lying around, not particularly worried about his next step.

At night, he sat around at Bombola's, looked at the pretty girls, and congratulated himself for not feeling any strong pressure to have them. On Sunday, he felt ill and had a sudden fear that he might become so weak that he wouldn't be able to call anyone for help and would be found dead in the apartment. His temperature rose and his condition worsened as the day went along; the grim scenario seemed a real possibility. Sunday night was his deadline on whether to commit to the show. As it got on toward midnight, he felt it was impossible to get out of bed and reach the telephone. Fifteen minutes before the appointed hour, struggling, as if he were moving through heavy syrup, he made it to his feet and somehow dialed Clement Hartog's number.

"I'm sick as a dog," he whispered, "but count me in."

"Oh, I'm so thrilled!" said Hartog, with the candor that had endeared him to Gurney. "Wait till mother hears the news."

Once Gurney had recovered, the three collaboraters decided to have dinner together to celebrate the beginning of their new venture. Gurney thought his two new friends might enjoy a visit to Lumpy's, a colorful bar and restaurant on the same street as his old precinct where homicide dicks and second-rate criminals alike tended to congregate. Hartog had promised to bring Essie along, but when he arrived, he was alone.

"Quite frankly," he said, "she's a little afraid to meet you. I think she'd prefer to demonstrate beforehand what she can do with your dialogue. I don't delude myself. She's probably a little sensitive about her son's being the director—and feels she might not have gotten the part on her own."

"That's preposterous," said Gurney. "I've heard she's marvelous."

"She is," said Hartog, close to tears. "And she'll go to hell and back for us in this show."

Welles, dapper and freshly barbered, showed up with the lovely woman he had brought to Bombola's.

"Since the last time you saw me," he said, his arms around her, "I've fallen madly in love with Tippy here, and we're to be married as soon as the show opens. But I've explained to her that I really can't concentrate on our romance while I'm working. And she understands."

Tippy smiled weakly, but it seemed to Gurney that she might not have been quite so understanding. Gurney, who knew the menu by heart, recommended Soup N'Beef, a heavily grueled stomach-liner of a dish much favored by the hardworking detectives.

"Is it any good?" asked Welles. "I've got to be careful with my eating when I'm working on a show."

"It's first-rate," said Gurney.

As he broke off a piece of the restaurant's popular corn bread, some shots rang out, causing his new friends to duck down instinctively in their seats.

"There's no cause for alarm," he assured the shaken group. "The rounds you just heard are from an adjacent firing range where the dicks take their practice once a week. Whenever I eat at Lumpy's I have a fantasy in which bullets slip through the walls and cut me down at the table."

"Do you think it's possible it might happen now?" asked Welles, who seemed terribly concerned with his physical condition. "Maybe we ought to move to another restaurant."

"No, no, it's safe," said Gurney. "Nobody's been shot here in weeks."

Tippy was interested in knowing about several men at the bar.

"Are they criminals or police?" she asked. She seemed excited by either possibility.

Gurney said that they were homicide dicks in plainclothes. The short stocky one in the group was Detective Gatti, who was known to be quick on the trigger and had more "kills" than anyone else in the Bureau. Though he had made a persuasive case for each incident, the Department kept a close eye on him. Several of his superiors considered him a walking grenade.

"It's good to know people like that," said Welles.

"When I get angry," said Hartog, who seemed to feel that his masculinity had been questioned, "I really lose my head."

A huge man in a Navy pea jacket walked up to the bar, ordered a beer, and then waved toward the table.

"Hey, Gurns," he shouted, "how they hangin'?"

After acknowledging him with a nod, Gurney explained to his friends that the man was a two-bit hood named Kicker who liked to hang around cops.

"There's quite a community of interest between the two groups. The hoods are fascinated by police, the way kids are by star athletes. The really important mobsters don't come in here, just the fringe types."

He said that Kicker was an expert foot-fighter. His style was to bump into someone, back away with his hands up in apology, saying, "Excuse me, fella, I didn't mean any harm," and then lash out with one of his feet and smash the man's jaw.

Kicker approached the table and said: "I heard you left Homicide, Gurns. What's the matter, getting too good for us?"

"Beat it, Kicker," Gurney said, looking the man in the eye. "Try any kicks and you're dead meat."

"Okay, okay," said Kicker, backing away with his hands up apologetically. "Pardon me for breathing."

"You handled that beautifully," said Tippy.

"It didn't take much . . . but thanks."

"I thought he was going to kick," said Welles, his brows knitting in fear. "I was sure of it."

"That's funny," said Hartog. "I knew he wasn't."

"Listen, Paul," said Welles, with a boyish and somewhat appealing grin, "if you had an argument with your collaborators, you wouldn't punch us out, would you?"

"Of course not," said Gurney. "I'm not really a fighter. But being in Homicide, you pick up a few tricks here and there."

"Well, that's a relief," said Welles. "Because sometimes collaborators don't get along. In the heat of a show, I mean. And you're probably strong enough to beat the shit out of me."

The next morning, Clement Hartog called Gurney and said that the first order of business was getting a producer to back the show. He spoke in the style of a man who had once been highly emotional and had taught himself to reason and to keep his passions in check.

"I don't delude myself," he said. *Violencia* is a tough nut. It doesn't have a star in the conventional sense. The composer comes out of tent shows and has been off the scene for many years, and the subject in many ways is abrasive and not your usual musical comedy fare."

"How about me?" said Gurney. "An unknown librettist."

"Somehow I don't think that's hurting us, Paul. All I know is that I believe in the basic material."

He said that he had reviewed the list of producers who might be available, canceled out most of them, and decided the best candidate was Philip Undertag, a man Gurney had never heard of before.

"What shows has he done?" Gurney asked, realizing it was no doubt presumptuous of him, of all people, to be asking this question.

Hartog said that Undertag had produced a dozen or more shows thus far and had never brought in a single hit. On the other hand, he was a square shooter, had a great deal of money, and was known never to quit on a project. "I don't want someone walking out on us before we've gotten off the ground," he explained.

Additionally, Undertag had varied interests, such as the ownership of a theatrical costuming company—and would be useful in getting out-of-town and Broadway bookings for *Violencia*.

"One more thing," said Hartog. "He knows Essie from her Vienna days. He adores her and understands that even though she's never done a big show, she is ready to stand this town on its ear."

"Well then, it's all right with me," said Gurney.

He was delighted that Hartog always seemed to consult him on an equal basis—as though Gurney himself had a wealth of background in show business.

The three collaborators met the producer the following day in the Undertag Building; in his travels about the city's downtown area, Gurney, for some reason, had never noticed the imposing structure.

Undertag was a stocky fellow who spoke somewhat haltingly; at each gap in the conversation, he would smile, take two corners of his wide slacks in his hands, and do a curtsy. It surprised Gurney to see that Clement Hartog, in speaking to the producer, was terribly deferential in his manner. He took a chair that was quite low to the ground, which somehow minimized the celebrated director's importance and made Undertag, standing behind his walnut desk, appear to be a figure of great eminence.

"I believe we've got a whale of a show, Mr. Undertag," said Hartog. "If you back us, have a little patience and faith in us—although I can't guarantee it—I think we can hand you a hit."

It upset Gurney to see the great director reduce himself in this manner. Nor could he for the life of him see why he felt the need to do so.

Undertag, to his credit, did not use Hartog's toadying manner to any particular advantage.

"I believe in you fellows," he said, "but even though I have plenty of money, I really don't like to put it at risk. I'll produce your show, but we'll have to get some outside dough. And my question is, where's it coming from?"

"That's the most ridiculous and insulting thing I've ever heard," said Norman Welles, leaping in with knitted eyebrows and terrible fury. "I myself can guarantee one hundred and fifty thousand dollars. Have your secretary get society's Betty Fiscus on the phone immediately. She is a friend of mine and is good for another fifty thou right there."

"It's all right with me," said Undertag, holding his hands aloft, giggling and doing his trademark curtsy.

Gurney was proud of Welles for standing up to the producer in a direct no-nonsense manner. He envied the composer, too, for being able to express himself openly and with such conviction.

Undertag's secretary made the call and came back with the information that Betty Fiscus was touring the Greek islands and could not be reached.

"That's a pity," said Welles. "The breaks are going against us. Because I'm sure that if I had gotten to her, Betty would have immediately fired off a check for the fifty. I played her some of my song ideas for the show and she got so excited she wet herself."

Though obviously he had an opening, Undertag declined to press his momentary advantage over Welles. As a result, Gurney began to think of the producer as a fine gentleman.

"All right, boys," said Undertag, "let's not concern ourselves with money at the moment. I'm producing the show. Let me worry about it. What's much more important is that we don't have a word down on paper. How do we know we can put on a show for the fall season? You fellows can use my offices, my facilities, and let's see if we can get the sucker written before we go any further."

"That sounds mighty fair to me, Mr. Undertag," said Clement Hartog, an odd folksy note creeping into his cultivated European delivery. "That all right with you boys?"

Welles nodded his assent. Gurney, of course, went along, and there were handshakes all around. Undertag said he had to leave, but that the three collaborators could remain in the office and begin right away if they liked. He did a sign-off curtsy at the door.

As soon as he was gone, Welles sat down at his desk and began putting through expensive long-distance calls to remote parts of the globe such as Bombay and Kuala Lumpur. Gurney thought it insensitive of Welles to take advantage of Undertag's offer in such an obvious manner; but on the other hand he admired the composer's flair and theatricality. He seemed to be calling brokers around the world who had made fortunes of money for him and berating them for not making more. Welles had a way of insulting people directly and getting away with it. Gurney shuddered to think what might have happened if the composer had tried that style on some of his old mates in Homicide.

While Welles was on the phone to Gstaad, the ex-dick asked Clement Hartog why he had been so deferential in dealing with Philip Undertag.

"Oh, was I?" said Hartog, wheeling about, less in surprise than as though he were an actor conveying surprise.

'Yes," said Gurney. "And it puzzled me, because you're so much more important than he is."

"You really think I was acting too respectful to him?" said Hartog, this time in genuine surprise. "Well, maybe I was. I'll watch it next time."

"How much would you fellows say I'm worth?" asked Welles when he had finished making his calls. "Go ahead, take a guess."

Hartog said half a million. Gurney had been living on the equivalent of detective's pay and was dazzled by the number. He said he had no idea.

"Four million two," said Welles, boyishly enthusiastic. "But if I don't watch it," he said, his mood switching to anger, "these bastards will let it slip down the drain. I just bring this up to indicate that I don't really have to do this show and can easily retire. But I love it, and it will be good to get my name up there in lights again."

When Hartog suggested that the trio get right down to work, Welles smiled exultantly, stretched, and said: "Look, fellows, this has been a great day for us. We've got a producer, we've got a hit on our hands. I'm just too excited to work. I say we adjourn for today and get a fresh start in the morning. I've got a little doll—well, hell, you met Tippy—and I'm dying to take her to dinner. I'm crazy about you two guys and I just hope that each of you gets to experience what I'm going through—really being in love."

Hartog laughed softly to himself and seemed to stroke an imaginary beard.

"All right, let's do that," he said wearily. "We'll get a fresh start in the morning."

Welles then looked around and appeared to notice Undertag's handsome suite of offices for the first time.

"What a terrific place to get laid."

He let the remark hang in the air a bit, then added, with an endearing chuckle: "What's wrong with me! I've got a fourteen-room town house for that. And besides, I'm in love with one of the greatest little gals in history. And she's smart as a whip, too."

Scene 2

They assembled the next day at Undertag's office. When they'd had their coffee and Danish pastries, Clement Hartog pushed the table back and said: "How to begin! It's vitally important in this project to make the right start. Otherwise, it could be costly."

"I don't care what anyone says," said Welles, his knees drawn up to his chest. "I think this will make one helluva musical."

"You don't know it," the composer said to Gurney, "but I've had my eye on this property for five years. I didn't contact you earlier because, who knows, you might have demanded a fortune for the basic material and really stuck it to me. And I wanted to get this great man, Clement Hartog, interested too. So this is a tremendously important day for me. Not that I have to be here. I could be out writing specialty songs for nightclub singers at five grand a crack. Maybe not in the States, but they love me in St. Tropez."

Lips pursed, looking somewhat gray and ashen, Clement Hartog said: "Quite frankly, gentlemen, I'm not sure I have a precise way to get rolling."

The three sat in silence for a few minutes. Gurney tried to appear in deep thought, but was not actually thinking.

"Look," said Welles, getting to his feet, "I think we're in trouble. Maybe you can't do a show on this subject. Maybe Undertag was right to be cautious. Fellows, I'm crazy about you two guys, but I'm pulling out. It's nothing personal, I hope we can remain friends and maybe even do a show together someday, but I know a turkey when I see one. I'll probably get singled out personally and get blasted by the critics, and I just don't know if I can take that. I'm not as young as I used to be and I don't have that many chances left."

Clement Hartog chuckled softly and patted Welles' knee.

"Norman, be a little patient. We're just getting started. I think we can lick it."

Gurney could see clearly that Hartog was going to be the strength and guiding force of the team.

"Look," said Welles, brows bunched together, eyes on fire, "I'm crazy about this material. I'm the one who brought it to you and kept it alive for five years and don't you ever forget it. I'll fight like a tiger for this show if I see there's a chance. But I just can't afford a flop, that's all. Just one of them and I'm out of the business and no one will ever work with me again. This is it for me, fellas. You, Paul, can go back to Homicide, and Clement here will have a million offers. Who'd ever collaborate with me if *Violencia* went down the drain?"

"Well, shall we just get on with it?" said Hartog patiently. "What's the beginning?"

They sat in silence again, Gurney thinking only of the deep, grave, almost Olympian concentration of Clement Hartog.

"Look, fellas," said Welles after a minute or so. "I can't work this way. I'm a composer, you guys are writers. I'm going back to my town house to work. I'll try some stuff on my own. As soon as you fellows have something, shoot it over to me and I'll put songs to it. That's the only way I can function. I did that on my last show, *Finally, Love,* and it worked beautifully, even though the show got killed for being ahead of its time. I knew how to fix it, but the writer was the world's worst sonofabitch and wouldn't give an inch. I sued his ass off, but don't worry, Paul, I'm not going to go after you in court. It was not that bad an experience, because at least the critics singled me out for praise on my score. When I saw that, I said fuck the show, at least I made out."

"Maybe it's not a bad idea for you to go off by yourself," said Hartog. "Paul and I will work alone for a while and see what happens. If we break through, we'll call you."

Gurney was touched each time the great director called him by his first name; also, he thought it was remarkable that he was able to be so patient with Welles, who, to use the kindest description, was behaving like a spoiled child.

"Good luck, fellas," said Welles, grinning with delight as though he had been let out of school early. "And I still say we've got a helluva chance."

"Paul," he said, his arm around Gurney "you're brilliant, and from what I've seen you can fart ideas."

When Welles had left, Gurney felt a little jittery, as though it might be up to him to concoct a wonderful notion on the spot. But Hartog's gentle, thoughtful, easygoing style calmed him down—and in some mysterious way, the two began, haltingly, to block out a plan for the show. Quite naturally, it would be located in the interior of a big-city homicide bureau, one known to have an outrageously high crime rate, and, as a consequence, an atmosphere more violent than virtually any other department in the country. The main character (to be played by Essie Hartog—although this was not stated but more or less implied by the two collaborators) would be the Chief of Homicide, a man wedded to the old, tough, head-cracking approach to criminal injustice. The key relationship would be that between the Chief and his son, also a homicide dick attached to the Bureau, but convinced there was another, more humane style of dealing with hoods. The basic machinery of the story would involve the war between them, the young detective's inevitable victory, and the tragedy of the Homicide Chief's Lear-like decline.

A key story line would involve a murderer on the loose in the city, one whose victims were all dry-cleaning personnel. He would turn out to be an attractive young black dick in the department. The decision on how to deal with him would bring into focus the schism between the Chief and his son, the former insisting on harsh punitive measures, the detective son favoring a search for understanding: What were the societal forces that turned a nice young dick into a killer who took out his wrath on pants-pressers?

A subplot would involve an adulterous situation in which one homicide dick violates another's wife, rubbing salt on the wound by using a police riot baton during sex, and the wife's eventual admission (ideally in song and dance) that it was the first time she had been able to achieve satisfaction in bed, and that if only her pigheaded husband had understood this, there would never have been a marital infidelity.

The collaborators agreed that it was all terribly touchy and might be horrendous on stage if not handled with extreme delicacy. Still, the material was worthwhile and deserved to be shown. It was their hope as well that the proper use of singing and dancing would take some of the edge off the content. Gurney knew that Hartog, for all of his international reputation, had hitherto been associated only with light comedy. Why then would the director want to enter such a tough and gamy arena?

"What the hell, Paul," he said. "I want to do something I can be proud of. Sure I'm nervous—it's an entirely different ball game for me. But by Christ, I think this show has something to say, and I want to help say it."

"What we have to do," said Hartog after an exhilarating but exhausting day, "is to get Norman involved. Can we take another minute and decide on a number we'd like him to get started on?"

The two thought a while and decided that a good beginning would be an atmospheric "umbrella" piece, to be sung—and danced—by the dicks. They agreed to use "Homicide" as a working title. The number would convey the dicks' feelings about the work they did, their fears, what they enjoyed about it, what it was that attracted them to their grisly occupation. As a model, Hartog said, it would be a good idea to keep in mind the wonderful "Tradition" number that got *Fiddler on the Roof* off to such a rousing start.

"I'll call Norman tonight and have him come down tomorrow morning," said Hartog. "I think we've made significant progress today."

He seemed terribly weary, as though the day's effort had aged him. Gurney, aware of being a much younger man, feared for a moment that the director might have a heart attack. Nontheless, he asked Hartog if he would like to go out and have a drink.

"I'd love to, but I'll have to call Mother and tell her to hold dinner."

Gurney was surprised that Hartog actually lived with his mother, but guessed that it was simply a temporary arrangement that would last only for the duration of the show.

Over drinks, Hartog corrected this notion and said that, as a matter of fact, he had always lived with his mother. At one period of his life, he'd had grave doubts about this arrangement, wondering if perhaps it it was an indicator of homosexual leanings. But some psychoanalytic sessions—several of which were attended by Essie—had cured him of that line of thinking.

"We just happen to have a very good thing going," he said, "and I don't think I could ever leave her side."

He said that in each show he directed, invariably there was one woman in the cast or crew who appealed to him.

"It's usually a middle-aged one with a terrific ass. At one point or another, generally on the road, I fuck her brains out, get it out of my system, and that tides me over until the next show. As far as I know, Essie knows about none of this, and I see no reason to throw it in her face.

"Unless you do," he added, with a sharp look at Gurney.

"I don't either," Gurney said.

From the first time he'd met the director, Gurney had wanted to tell him about his divorce, feeling somehow that the older man would be deeply understanding about it. Sensing that the moment was right, he described his ex-wife and said that although they had had a stormy marriage, he was afraid that in some curious way he was still a little bit in love with her.

"She has some qualities—theatrical ones, I guess you could call them—that I don't ever expect to find in another woman."

"How old is she?" asked Hartog.

It was a touchy question. Gilda Gurney had always been reluctant to reveal her true age, and Gurney, to his surprise, found himself loyally trimming off a few years and saying that she was thirty-two. Hartog, whose eyes watered at the drop of a hat, took in this information and then went over the brink into actual tears, saying: "Oh, you poor, poor bastard."

It was the first time Gurney had ever resented anything the man said or did.

"It's not that bad," he said, and then fell back on his coarse, detectivey style. "I get a lot of pussy."

"Oh, yeah," said Hartog, drying his eyes and reacting sharply. "Where?"

"Around town, here and there," said Gurney. "There are nests of them all over the city if you look hard enough."

He had been offended by Hartog's sympathy for him, which must have accounted for the sudden burst of feigned virility on his part. It took a while to get over Hartog's annoyingly tearful reaction to his marital breakup, but he did. He also knew that he would probably end up discussing his personal difficulties with Hartog again, thereby walking into the same trap.

The director was a fine and modest man, although it was probably his *look* of sympathy that was so effective. Was it possible that he wasn't particularly sympathetic, but was merely a great actor, able to *convey* sympathy without feeling a trace of it? Whatever the case, Gurney felt he had a valuable friend in his new life. Hartog's involvement was the main reason Gurney was willing to go ahead with *Violencia*.

It was of greater importance than the promise of millions.

At Undertag's office the next morning, the director told Gurney that he had phoned Welles at home only to find that the composer had gone off to Puerto Vallarta. But he had tracked him down at the pricey vacation spot and gotten Welles' guarantee that he would plane in immediately for the meeting.

"He certainly does take good care of himself," said Hartog.

Gurney had been led to believe that the three of them would have a tight and intensive collaboration and was surprised that Welles had taken himself off to a tropical paradise just as the project was getting under way.

Welles arrived before long, lean, suntanned, and fit. After a moment or so, he had Gurney feeling guilty about having interrupted his Mexican hiatus.

"I've been working my ass off down there," he said, his forehead creased with anger. "The trick is to get up very early in the morning, compose until noon, and then you've got almost the entire day for waterskiing and attending to your health.

"My dad is in his nineties, which is a great factor on my side along the lines of longevity. I'm scared to death of dying and want to live as long as I possibly can."

Gurney sensed that Clement Hartog, too, felt a little sheepish about summoning Welles back. The director sketched in some of the progress they had made and then told Welles their idea for an opening homicide number.

"Cute," said Welles, but then he chuckled and shook his head with amused disbelief as though a child had made some outrageous error in basic logic.

"You fellows don't seem to understand. You can knock off a scene just like that, but a song is an entirely different kettle of fish. It takes a week of playing with it, then it has to be scored, orchestrated. . . . It's a thousand times more difficult than a scene. You expect me to come up with it, bam, one, two, three, just like that. I have to be alone, sometimes for days at a time. It might come to me in the middle of the night. I sweat and scrimp for every note and sometimes throw the whole thing out and begin again. I just don't understand you guys, and I don't think you're playing fair with me."

"Then take your time," said Hartog. "No one's rushing you."

"All right," said Welles. "I just can't permit anyone to break my balls, that's all."

On his way out, he patted Gurney's knee and flashed a genuinely delightful grin.

"It's not you, Paul," he said. "You're terrific."

The composer seemed to be a little frightened of Gurney, perhaps because of his background at the Bureau, plus Welles' extreme concern for his own physical well-being.

Gurney congratulated Hartog on his extraordinary patience with the composer.

"I'll bet that's the trick to being a great director," said Gurney. "I don't mean to offend, but that quality is probably every bit as important as talent."

"I'm not generally that patient," said Hartog. "I just hope it doesn't turn out that I'm behaving this way because my mother has the lead in the show."

Gurney told the director not to be so hard on himself.

"From all I've heard, your mom is a gifted actress and would have landed the police chief role even if the cards weren't heavily stacked in her favor."

"I hope so," said Hartog. "But I've got to keep the issue in mind continually."

Twenty minutes later, Welles called and said: "It was a bitch, but I cracked it. Can you fellows stop everything you're doing and come right uptown to hear it? It's the single greatest piece of work I've ever done. When I think that every once in a while I've looked upon myself as a washed-up guy . . ."

Gurney could imagine Welles shaking his head in disbelief.

"Well, the mind plays funny tricks sometimes," said Welles.

"I thought it would take him at least a week," said Gurney when the composer had hung up.

"He's full of shit," said Hartog. "You can write a song in five minutes."

He said it would probably set a bad precedent for them to stop everything and run right up to Welles' place just because the composer had called.

"Why the hell doesn't he come down here?"

But as Hartog spoke, Gurney noticed that the director was putting on his hat and coat.

Welles lived in a handsomely appointed brownstone in Greenwich Village, one that was immaculately kept but clearly had the touch of a decorator. On the walls were beautifully framed notices of the traveling tent shows Welles had done many years back, with passages related to his work blown up and underlined. This seemed in questionable taste to Gurney, but it was done on such a bold and unashamed scale that somehow it was acceptable. And there was no denying that the notices were awfully good, although for the most part he had gotten them in shows that were otherwise unsuccessful.

"Norman Welles' songs provide the single cheerful note in an otherwise dreary panorama of tedium," read a representative one, which Welles had posted prominently over a bricked fireplace. *"Would that the poor man had surrounded himself with some decent collaborators."*

The composer greeted them in a flowered silk kimono. He seemed in good spirits, although perhaps a bit more nervous than usual. He poured them drinks, sat them in comfortable chairs around a piano, and introduced a tiny, immaculately groomed and slightly humpbacked man named Tito Passionato as his piano-playing assistant—available to him day and night on an exclusive basis.

"Many of my ideas come to me at four in the morning," said Welles. "No matter how tired I am, I phone them in to Tito here, who is on constant round-the-clock call. I hum the section over the phone and he takes it down and commits it to paper. I pay him four-fifty a week for this, and believe me, it hurts. But I feel it's worth it when you consider what I eventually make on the songs—sometimes hundreds of thousands. Tito has no other life. If he were to let me down and not be around when I needed him I would see to it that he never got another job in the music business."

Tito smiled, but a bit unevenly, as though he were not entirely convinced it was the best of all possible arrangements for him. Still, he seemed determined to make the most of it.

Welles became increasingly jittery, steering the conversation around to economic policy during the Truman administration. Predictably, the exchange of comments was forced and somewhat clumsy.

"Are we going to hear the song?" Hartog asked after a while.

"Don't rush me," Welles shouted. "I can't be pushed around the way other composers can. I've had hits, big ones, too, and don't you forget it. So don't pull that on me."

Gurney was not happy to hear Welles take that tone with the great director, a man he now considered his friend.

"We'd both like to hear it," he said, supportively.

Welles produced a sound that came across as a combination of a chuckle and a snicker.

"Since when did you become an expert, Paul? Someone would think you'd done fourteen musicals."

The remark hit Gurney in a sensitive place: his total lack of experience. He felt his face heat up with anger. Welles must have sensed this and did an about-face.

"I'm kidding, Paul. And I can see you've taken my comment the wrong way. All I'm saying is that you've got remarkable instincts. It's as though you've been working on shows since you were a pup."

"Now, I called you guys up to hear a song," he said, smoothly shifting gears, "and you want to hear it. That's excellent thinking."

Tito played some background chords on the piano that seemed designed to lighten the atmosphere. When the chords unaccountably turned somewhat harsh and abrasive, Welles wheeled around in his chair.

"Easy, Tito, easy . . . much softer. Do you want them to hate what's coming up?"

Tito smiled blandly and made a correction, segueing into a gentler musical theme. As tough as Welles was with his assistant, Gurney sensed that he was also capable of being quite nice to him. Why else would the obviously talented man have stuck it out with the moody composer?

"Now look, fellas," said Welles, "what you're going to hear is so rough, such a preposterously early dummy of a song, that I ought to have myself shot for doing it for you. It's practically spitballing—and all it's designed to do is give you a taste, a *hint* of what it can be. I want you also to consider my voice, which is pathetic and thin and under constant strain. Try to imagine the song, Paul—especially you, since you have zero background in the field—try to imagine it with either Essie herself singing it, or a full chorus of men, backed up with heavy orchestration, woodwinds, flutes coming up at the right time, solid brass. And don't forget lights, makeup, the comforts of a modern, acoustically sound theatre, which Undertag better come up with, if he knows what's good for him. And Christ, I almost forgot. I'm no actor. This is a song that has to be directed. and I think we can all agree that we've got one of the all-time greats in that department, Mr. Clement Hartog."

He paused here, and looked over at the director as if expecting him to take a bow.

"In any case," Welles continued, "with all that behind the song, I guarantee you it will be tremendous and stop the goddamned show cold.

"Take it from the top, Tito, and play your heart out."

Welles began to sing a pretty melody. Gurney felt the composer had been much too critical of his voice. Though every bit as thin and reedy as Welles said it would be, it also came across as being authentic-sounding and therefore quite appealing. What troubled Gurney was that the lyric had nothing to do with homicide. It dealt instead with the joys of Paris—"not in the spring, not in the fall, not in the winter, but during the off-season." How in the world Welles could imagine a tribute to the City of Love being delivered by a stageful of homicide dicks in the detectives' bullpen was beyond Gurney, experience or no experience. He was certain, however, that Hartog would see immediately that the lyric had absolutely nothing to do with the show.

When Welles had finished the song, the composer leaned forward expectantly.

"What did you two guys think of it?"

Gurney averted his eyes, not daring to express an opinion.

To his surprise, Clement Hartog was silent for a moment, too, stroking that imaginary beard of his in solemn consideration.

"Let me hear it again," he said finally.

Gurney was startled by the director's failure to comment on the song's screamingly obvious lack of appropriateness. Either Hartog, once again, was being overly diplomatic, or else he had some absurdist scheme for the show that he hadn't discussed with Gurney.

Welles ran through the song again, and Gurney enjoyed it just as much the second time. It was, no question, a catchy tune, and it was fun listening to Welles' thin but romantic voice. But at the same time he was certain there was no way on earth it could be wedged into the detectivey musical.

"Now look," said Hartog, "I think you've written a brilliant number, Norman. But there are a couple of lines I have to seriously question."

"Which ones?" asked Welles in what seemed to be genuine shock.

"Well, quite frankly, the Paris-during-the-off-season reference," said Hartog. "What do you think, Paul?"

"I agree," said Gurney. "I admit I speak from total lack of experience, but I just don't see how you can imagine a group of homicide dicks—and believe me, I know these guys—giving a thought to Paris in the off-season. I don't think there's more than one dick in a bureau who's been to Paris in *any* season, and if he was, he'd be chasing a wise guy up the Eiffel tower. So it seems an odd way to get the show off the ground."

"I knew they would take that approach, didn't I, Tito?" Welles said to his assistant in an ominously calm voice. "Didn't I say they would come down hard on that aspect of the song?"

"You did, Mr. Welles."

"Well, all I can say, fellas, is that you're dead wrong. Now I've played ball with you guys up to now and I think you'll admit I've been a good boy. But when you tell me that song is shit, you really back me to the wall. Fellas, I *know* that song will score for us. I agree there may be a phrase or two of the lyric that isn't absolutely on the nose, but those are out-of-town fixes; I can do them in my sleep. Now you guys have just got to trust me. Goddammit, in my last show, *Finally, Love,* I took the entire chorus into the men's room and rehearsed a new second-act opening number in stealth, behind the director's back, and slipped the number by him, and it got healthy applause. The reviews of the show said we were garbage, but several of the critics singled that number out as having merit—and at least I wasn't completely killed the way the book writer and the director were.

"Now I'm really angry. You come in here, you listen to the song once, no orchestration, me with my thin, reedy voice—which incidentally has been under a lot of strain lately—and you expect it to sound like fucking *Aida*. I don't know what you guys want from me."

"What if you were to adjust the lyric," said Hartog calmly, "so that it referred to Precinct Nineteen in the off-season, instead of Paris? Would that work?"

Gurney followed the director's thinking, and although he didn't consider it an ideal solution, he felt that a song about a precinct in the off-season might just slip by and would have the advantage of an awfully pretty melody behind it.

"It won't wash musically," said Welles. "The entire construction will go down the drain, and I'll get killed in the reviews. I'd rather yank the entire show off the boards, and have all of us go down the tubes together—even though there's a chance that no one in the business will ever work with me again.

"Don't punch me in the mouth for this, Paul," he said, turning to Gurney, "but I'm not changing a word of that song. I can't. I'm just not built that way. I worked too hard on the goddamned thing."

Gurney thought that if Welles was really afraid of being smashed in the face, it took a certain amount of courage for him to be speaking this way.

"I guess that's it," Gurney said to Hartog as the two shared a cab uptown.

"I'm afraid so," said Hartog. "We could take it to another composer, but I suppose it's not morally right, since Norman really did originate the project. Besides, he'd sue our asses off. Norman loves to sue. He *lives* to sue.

"It's a damned shame, too," Hartog continued, "because the sonofabitch really does have ability—that melody, for example—but he obviously hates to work."

Gurney suggested that even if Welles made some adjustment in the lyric, the song would continue to be way off target.

"I disagree with you there," said Hartog. "Of course, it's not our precise notion. But I just don't think people listen that hard to lyrics, and it's my view that we'd probably get by with it and come in with something highly adequate."

Gurney thought back to the few shows he had seen and had to admit that whenever there was a stageful of people with strong voices, singing and dancing, the net effect was pleasing and it didn't seem to matter what they were singing about.

Hartog asked the cab to stop at a midtown address and apologized for not inviting Gurney upstairs.

"Essie is a terrible housekeeper, and quite frankly I'm ashamed to have people visit. But it's so bloody upsetting. I'm crazy about the material in this show, and no matter how many big commercial hits I have in the future, this is the one I feel America ought to see."

Gurney was surprised to find that he wasn't quite as disappointed about the aborted project as he thought he might be. Of course, there was a chance he would never again get to work on a major musical comedy. In a sense, however, the work on *Violencia* had been inter-ruptive; he had not quite gotten his fill of the simple, uncluttered bachelor life he had been enjoying. The death of the show meant he could get right back to it.

That night, he bought a new corduroy bedspread and spent the evening rolling around and luxuriating on it. Just as he was about to fall asleep, he got a call from his ex-wife saying she had heard he was involved in a new musical and insisted on going to the opening night on his arm.

"I've got to have your decision right now as to whether you'll take me, Paul, because I need a lot of advance time so that I can buy an evening gown. I feel I deserve it for the years I spent with you while you had that shitty job and weren't working on musicals. Don't ask me to explain any further. I just want to go, and I don't need any twenty-year-old bimbo cashing in on the deal."

Gurney said that he had not thought that far ahead, and as a matter of fact, there wasn't going to be a musical anyway.

"But even if there was—I admire and respect you, Gilda, but truthfully . . . looking at the whole picture . . . I'm not entirely sure I'd want to be with you that night."

"So there *is* somebody," said Gilda. "What's she like? Big tits, right?"

"I don't know what she's like," said Gurney, "because there isn't anybody at the moment. But there might be, a little further down the line . . . and I'd probably want to be with her. Would you want to go to an opening with me, knowing I'd prefer to be with someone else?"

"Absolutely," she said. "It's me or no one."

Was it his imagination, Gurney wondered, or was everyone suddenly speaking in song lyrics?

"Well, I can't give you an answer on the spot."

"All right, but you'd better hurry up and decide, one way or the other. I've got my eye on a gown, and I need lots of time to get it fitted.

"And if you decide against me," she said, altering her tone, "I may very well have to change a few of my own plans."

There was a definite threat in her voice as she said good-bye, and although Gurney could not imagine which plans she had in mind, he was concerned as to what they might be. He had always been a little afraid of Gilda, in a curious way, and this apprehension, even after the divorce, was still reflexively there. What could she be threatening him with? A divorce? They'd already had one. Now they'd *really* get divorced? Could she be hinting that she would fuck every one of his friends at the Bureau? Go down the list methodically, ticking them off one by one? The scenario was an old nightmarish fantasy of his, but the truth was, he had it pretty much under control now. If she did sail right through the list, it would have nothing to do with him. He would feel sorry for her, since obviously the act would have been one of desperation. Although you never knew—possibly she'd enjoy every second of it.

No doubt what troubled him more than anything was the possibility that she was saying something else: that they would never get together again. Ever. This was a dark thought. Because even though they had gone ahead with the legalities, he had never said a total and complete good-bye to Gilda Gurney. And he had always dreamed that they could, perhaps years later, somehow drift back together.

He did not know at the moment if he would take her to the opening. And though the whole issue was academic—it looked as if there would be no show to take her to—it bothered him considerably.

Scene 3

artog called first thing the next morning.

"I've got some good news for you, Paul. Our composer has decided to go along with us and change the lyric to 'I love *Precinct Nineteen,* not in summer, not in fall or winter, but in the off-season.' He has only one condition. At some point in the writing of the libretto, we have to make a change totally on his say, whether we want to or not, and no matter how firmly we are committed to whatever he wants changed. It can be the scene we love most in the show—ideally, he would *like* it to be the scene we love most. Norman admits this might be just a whim on his part, but he needs it for his ego. Anyway, I agreed to the arrangement on behalf of both of us. Needless to say, I'm thrilled, and I hope you are, too."

Gurney was not so sure he was thrilled. But he said he was and then hopped in a cab to join his two collaborators at Undertag's office. Welles was there, fresh and beaming. Gurney, to his surprise, was truly glad to see him. He was even more surprised to discover that he was caught up in emotion—and mysteriously close to tears—as Welles embraced him with a thin-armed bear hug. All of this was so much different from the Bureau where a dick would rather stick his head in an oven than get caught being sentimental. And where a

Gurney saw that he had made a mistake in being so fiercely honest with Miss Hottle and tried, unsuccessfully, to tease his way out of it.

"Ah, c'mon now, not even a little tiny bit, if you really dig down?"

"No, not a drop," she said, "no matter how far I dig down. And I think it's disgraceful that you have some of it in you."

Though she found Gurney suspect in his social thinking, Miss Hottle was kind to him in every way, lining up excellent tickets for hit shows, taking care of his meagre correspondence, and even sewing buttons on his one sports jacket. She was a curious contradiction and saw nothing wrong with taking part in a lunchtime protest for the homeless, then dashing right back to work for Undertag, whose vast property interests had led some to describe him as a piggish real estate hustler and world-class slumlord.

After his work on the *Violencia* libretto was finished for the day, Gurney would often linger at the office, sometimes wandering into Undertag's inner sanctum just to lounge around for a bit. Undertag had told Gurney to make himself at home in the office, and the ex-dick, behaving in a manner that wasn't typical of him, took advantage of the offer, smoking the producer's choice Havana cigars and taking sips of his vintage Scotch whiskey. On occasion, he would sit at Undertag's huge mahogany desk, swiveling about in his chair—and at other times he would kick off his shoes and sink into the producer's couch. The net effect was sexually arousing. It crossed his mind that he might make some sort of proposal to the woman who tidied up at the end of the day. But he held off. He just wasn't ready for cleaning-lady sex.

Not that he was was afraid of being arrested. If the woman were to call the police, that wouldn't be much of a problem—the dicks took care of their own. But they would certainly have a field day teasing him about his fancy new job in show business. They were merciless about anyone in the Bureau who was stuck-up and put on

airs. Gurney recalled the case of a certain detective in Art Fraud who
gave a party and made the mistake of hiring a uniformed waiter to
serve drinks; they practically rode him out of the Bureau for that
one. There was no question that Gurney's new line of work put him
in the fancy and too-good-for-the-rest-of-us category.

As for *Violencia* itself, Gurney couldn't quite tell with any
certainty exactly how it was going. A distracting presence was
Undertag's assistant, the distinguished-looking, always nattily
dressed Tom Toileau, who operated as a kind of watchdog against
the use of harsh or abusive language that he felt would drive audiences and theatre party people away from the show. This put him
in conflict with Gurney and Hartog, who had decided to be forceful
in dealing with the show's language, since detective talk was by its
nature strong and colorful. A no-holds-barred approach seemed the
proper way to proceed. Actually, Gurney was not as much of a
stickler in this area as Clement Hartog, who seemed to be trying to
prove he was tough and ballsy after a career hitherto thrown over
to successful but more or less light family fare. (Indeed, one critic
had referred to him derisively as "Mr. Frothy.")

Gurney had told Clement Hartog about a certain old-timer
of a detective who used the word "doody" quite often, saying "Doody
on you" to other detectives around the Bureau, to suspects, and even
to puzzled everyday citizens encountered during routine investigations.
He was a rugged dick from the old school, and though no one ever
called him this to his face, his nickname around the Bureau was
"Detective Doody." The question before the two collaborators was
whether to feature the word in the show, Gurney not caring one way
or the other and Hartog, after musing over it, taking a strong position.

"It adds texture to the show, and I see no reason to back
away from it."

Toileau, quite typically, drifted by during the discussion and
said, "I couldn't help overhearing you two fellows. And all I can say
is why in the hell do you want to lose them out there?"

He made it clear that he wasn't objecting to the word on a personal basis.

"I myself have used the word 'doody' on more than one occasion, and I wouldn't pull back from using it at a cocktail party, if the situation warranted it. I've used 'titty' and 'bum,' too, many times, as a boy and as a grown man. But that does not mean I would want to see those terms used in the theatre. I just say to you that they've come in to town for a good time, they're pulling for you, they ask for so very little—why in the hell drive them out?"

"I disagree with you, Tom," said Hartog.

The director then brought into play a special authority that comes with having registered an enormous number of successes in the past. That his triumphs were essentially light and fluffy ones was beside the point—and may have even been a strength in Toileau's family-oriented eyes.

"I think 'doody' works for us," the director continued. "Now if you were telling us to avoid using 'doody' as the theme for a musical number, I'd go along and follow you there. Music does enhance theatrical values, and with all of the brass and violins behind it the effect might be just too strong. But otherwise, I don't think it's anything to back away from."

"Okay, fellas," said Toileau. He was quite reasonable and good-natured in defeat. "Doody it is, and I'll defer to you boys as creators. I just don't think there's any theatrical gold there. You're giving up a lot for a little."

Gurney did not feel that Toileau had been in the least bit intractable. Nontheless, after he left, Hartog was clearly annoyed.

"There are times when I think we picked the wrong producers. They're telling *me* what works in the theatre," he said, with a contemptuous shrug.

"Doody stays!" his powerful directorial voice boomed out. "Now let's get on with it."

Gurney was all for moving along, but the work had a frustrating way of not going forward. Most of the time, Gurney felt it was his inexperience that was getting in the way; but he also had a hunch that another factor was Hartog's extreme care and concern with being absolutely right on each decision. At first, Gurney found this appealing—he was allied with a man who strove for perfection; how could this fail to make him happy? On other occasions, Gurney allowed himself to think that Hartog was a trifle indecisive. No sooner would the team agree on a sequence, with Gurney poised to record it, than Hartog would say: "Now hold off a minute, Paul, maybe we're going off half-cocked. Let's think about it."

Gurney, who in so many ways was hanging on to the great director's coattails, would sit back and see clearly, of course, that there was cause for reexamination. The result was that after a month of effort, the two had tons of ideas but didn't have a single page of the libretto on paper. This was troubling to Gurney, who tended to have a quantitative approach to life—i.e., the man with two pages of libretto was better off than the man with none—though he realized it led him to preposterous conclusions, such as that someone with four marriages was much better off than the individual with only one. He did not need a cheap analysis having to do with penis size to account for these feelings. He had them—that was enough.

Still, the two really did have a rough scheme for the libretto; the first act, for example, would end with a major song-and-dance production number in which the handsome rogue dick is apprehended and hauled into the Bureau. The general theme of the number would be "I Think We've Got Him," the dicks singing and dancing in a manner that highlighted the division in the group—one faction wanting to beat the living shit out of him, the other choosing to examine the childhood and societal factors that forced him to become a killer of pants-pressers.

Hartog felt they had the finale licked as well. Almost inevitably, it had to be a musical number in which the Homicide Chief—

played, of course, by Essie Hartog—packs up and leaves the Bureau while her enlightened son, chosen to take over, looks on, torn between love and hatred for his defeated dad.

"I know where we're driving," said Hartog. "If only I had a clue as to how to get there."

At the musical end, Welles kept pushing forward, although the two collaborators rarely saw him. They would sketch in notions for songs and Welles, after a few days, would phone them so that they could rush over and listen to what he had. The songs were unfailingly quite appealing and attractively varied in rhythmic approach. Irritatingly, however, they went off in lyrical directions that, to put it charitably, had nothing to do with the show. As an example, Gurney and Hartog felt that a sequence involving the brutal grilling of an aggravated-assault-and-battery suspect should take the form of a duet:

Detective (singing): Did you kick the victim's ass?
Suspect (singing): Nosiree, nosiree.
Detective: Did you smack him in the head?
Suspect: No, I didn't.

Welles' answer to their suggestion was a number about the delights of ragtime Broadway during the twenties. Hartog thought there were strong comedic possibilities in the activities of Detective Centro, who invested hours of his time peering in through hotel room transoms to watch hookers giving blow jobs to out-of-town johns. But Welles' song, curiously, and maddeningly, dealt with a disappointed young man who passes a restaurant, looks through the window, and sees his lost love "dining with somebody new."

The two collaborators then came up with what they felt was a can't-miss possibility for a number involving a detectives' dance, at the height of which a young rookie prankster shows up with a nicely attired dead body from the morgue as his partner. Welles' musical attack on the idea dealt with a small-town girl who can't keep her feet still and feels compelled to leave her waitressing job in Topeka, hitchhike to New York, and pursue her deam of becoming a Broadway star. A tried-and-true notion, decent enough, but drastically out of sync with the scene it was intended to incorporate in music.

Hartog, and Gurney as well, to a lesser extent, battled the composer on each of the songs, but the process was wearying, and even though Welles backtracked a bit now and then, the effect was discouraging. In each case, Welles would say he knew the lyrics were a little sketchy but that repairs would be simple. If they'd just let him go about his business, they'd see that he would be able to make the corrections easily, most of them light, insignificant, out-of-town fixes.

"Being new to this and understandably bewildered," he would tell Gurney, "you probably feel let down from time to time and don't see how a show like this—with all its bits and pieces— can ever come together. But you'll be amazed when you see how it does."

Hartog's fights with the composer over the songs became less spirited. Gurney felt he could see the energy leaking out of him. After a while, it was as if Hartog had blacked out the musical problem entirely.

"Let's just attend to our side, Paul," he said. "If we nail the libretto, and it's good and strong, the rest will fall into line."

Oddly enough, it was Gurney whose feelings welled up one day and who snapped.

"Look, Clement, the goddamned songs just don't fit the show we're trying to put on stage. They're all light love songs, and it's crazy to go along this way. With all due respect to your vast experience and my lack of any."

"Do you think I ought to bring this to a head?" the director asked, sadly.

"Yes," said Gurney. He was convinced for a change that he was right—and consequently not at all shaky about taking the strong position.

The two held a showdown meeting with Welles. The director hemmed and hawed and was extremely polite and diplomatic. But finally he suggested that Welles might need some help.

"Not on your melodies, Norman, which God knows are beautiful . . . but on the lyrics."

Gurney gripped the sides of his chair, expecting a storm of protest, and was surprised to see Welles seem to collapse into himself, his eyes wet, his voice choked and barely audible.

"Oh, my God," he said, as if a confession had been slapped out of him. "My *God.* You can't do this to me. I've got millions and don't need this show the way another fellow might . . . you, Paul, as an example, who probably don't have a pot to piss in . . . but do you realize what you're suggesting?"

He begged for another chance to show what he could do.

"I think we owe it to him, Clement," said Gurney, who was touched by the composer's apparent collapse.

The two agreed to give Welles another try, but when they left the office that night, they were not optimistic about his chances for success, his first efforts being so obviously wide of the mark.

The next day, Welles called them down to his town house and sang a number, to be delivered by an older man in the Bureau to his young boy, called, "Son, Be a Cop for Your Pop." The thrust of the song had to do with the father's urging his son to follow in his footsteps and to give up his dream of a career in retailing. It was a simple, somewhat sentimental tune which did nothing but state the same theme over and over. But it had a mawkish honesty to it and the two had to admit that although they weren't planning such a sequence, at least it had a remote connection to the show.

Gurney gave the composer a hug. Hartog chucked him playfully on the chin.

"I knew you could do it, you sonofagun. Why have you been holding out on us?"

Welles hung his head and accepted the praise with that terribly appealing grin of his. The three then sat down and had a celebratory drink.

Later, after leaving the composer's place, Hartog said: "I think I know the secret with this guy. You've just got to give him a kick in the ass once in a while."

Gurney, who had been elated, sobered up quickly and suggested that apart from the new song, which they would probably end up not using, they were not in much better shape than when they had walked into the meeting.

"What about the other songs?" he said. "I know it looks as if I'm focused on the dark side, but they just don't agree with the rest of the show. It's as though they were written for another musical."

"Sonofabitch," said Hartog, smacking himself on the head. "I never thought of that. I'll bet the bastard really did write them for another show and is slipping them to us, one by one, to save work for himself."

Despite this fear, the two pushed on with *Violencia,* mostly because of Hartog's dogged urging. Gurney considered just quitting cold, not showing up one morning and going back to his routine of sitting around in the apartment he loved. But he felt he owed allegiance to the director, who seemed to be aging at a rapid clip right before Gurney's eyes.

One morning, Hartog became obsessed with the possibility that the producers were just jerking them around for the fun of it.

"Why do you feel that way?" asked Gurney.

"I don't know . . . it's just a feeling I have. We're in here each day, busting our butts. And what have they done, really, except let us use their offices? The sonsofbitches don't have the faintest inkling of what they're sitting on with this property."

"But we don't have have a word on paper. How could they be expected to proceed with plans for the show?"

"Fuck it," said Hartog. "We've given them enough of a taste to go by." He suggested getting Welles down the next morning and having a cards-on-the-table meeting with the producers.

The three collaborators joined Undertag and his staff the next morning in the producer's office, Gurney experiencing a pleasing sense of solidarity as he sat with his two partners opposite the producing team. He had never felt that close to Welles, yet on this occasion he found himself exchanging winks with the handsome composer as the meeting got under way.

Representing the producers were Undertag, of course; Toileau; a fledgling producer associate of Undertag's named Greg Mandarin, and Miss Hottle, who took notes. Undertag kicked off the meeting.

"Let's be as frank as we can, boys, because we want to stay friends, even if this project goes down the drain, as all my others have."

Toileau then took over and said he sensed the writers were displeased by the lack of effort on the producer's part.

"But fellows, all I for one know about the show is that you're highlighting the word 'doody.' As I've said quite openly, I don't see how you're going to hold an audience with that."

"May I put in something?" said Hartog, quite modestly, but firmly, causing Gurney to relax—his team was about to come to bat. Legs crossed in an almost feminine manner, and hunched over as if to defend himself, the director proceeded to deliver a thrilling speech worthy of the Founding Fathers. He sketched in the forces that had first led him to *Violencia,* the reasons he felt the play was important and *had* to be done, not only for audiences but for the welfare of the nation. He praised his two colleagues, making the point that although he'd had differences with Welles in particular, he had a new respect and the highest regard for the composer.

"I can't tell you how impressed I am with the effort Norman is putting out."

His speech was delivered with an open-faced, naked candor and a tremendous sense of integrity, all of this coupled with the dignity and presence that only a man long schooled in the theatre arts can muster.

"Frankly, gentlemen," he said in conclusion, "I don't think you fellows have played fair with us."

So great was the impact of his speech that when it was over, each person in the room rose and applauded for what must have been a full thirty seconds.

At this point, Undertag, who was not without a rough-hewn Broadway wit, said: "I hope the show gets this much applause out of town."

Then he added quickly: "Look, I'm going to say right now that you have a point, Clement, and that you've really impressed me. I had no idea you boys were thinking along those lines. Now I intend to produce this show, but you on your part have to agree that you must give me a show to produce. When you do, we'll take it from there."

Toileau said he agreed with Undertag, and there was a general sense among the three collaborators that it had been useful to clear the air. However, Gurney was not quite sure whether anything had actually been accomplished. Soon after the meeting, he mentioned his uncertainty to Hartog.

"What did he really say, Clement?"

"Damned if I know," said the director, who, following his oration, appeared to be exhausted, if not on the verge of having a heart attack.

"I smell a rat," said Welles. "I think we ought to make secret calls around town to other producers and protect ourselves against the conniving of these guys."

The composer's remarks, typically, were self-serving, but Gurney found that on this occasion, he didn't mind them. Obviously, Welles' idea served his own interests, too.

"I don't know, Norman," said Hartog. "Maybe we're jumping the gun. My feeling is the man is sincere and will proceed if given a good shove. It's up to us to stay tied to his ass."

Just before Gurney left the office that day, Greg Mandarin took him aside.

"Gee, I'm awfully sorry to hear that you fellows don't really trust us. We had no idea you felt that way . . . and you're wrong.

"Incidentally," he said, gently ushering Gurney into his office, "I'm behind your 'doody' concept."

The gentle, soft-spoken little fellow locked the door.

"Look, I sort of work for Undertag," he said, "but what the hell, I've got to look out for myself, too, don't I? What I'm about to say is would you be interested in doing another musical if this one were to close, which quite frankly you've got to think seriously about in this game. It would focus on the amazingly spry and colorful characters in Virginia nursing homes. My mother is in one of them and has agreed to cooperate and be available for meetings. The Broadway audience is aging rapidly, and this would be right down the pike for them. We could set to work immediately on it, the second *Violencia* goes under, instead of going to those awful self-pitying parties that are thrown right after the closing notices are posted. And believe me, I've been to quite a few of them. You could leap right into another project, richer, deeper, with better collaborators and with me at the helm, no offense to the boys you're working with."

Mandarin said that if Gurney didn't mind and had some free time, they could have meetings on the new show in stealth, at slow times during the preparation of *Violencia,* and perhaps try to block out a few scenes.

What Mandarin was proposing should really have been infuriating—the idea of working behind his employer's back and stealing Gurney's services in cold blood. But Gurney was only slightly offended. In a way, Mandarin, for all of his duplicity, was paying him a compliment. After all, Gurney was obviously untrained in the business and had yet to get his first page written, much less his first show credit. Still, he backed off, for many reasons: The characters in Virginia nursing homes really didn't interest him, no matter how spry and colorful they were—and he honestly thought *Violencia* had a chance, if it ever got before the public. And what was he supposed to do—just casually set aside his loyalty to Clement Hartog? What would that say about him? Obviously, Mandarin did not know his customer. And he saw no reason to thank the man.

"I just don't think so," he said, and started for the door.

"Good Christ," said a panicked Mandarin, "you're not about to go in there and tell Undertag, are you? If he gets wind of this, after the break he gave me in show business, out I go on my ass and I'll have to start all over again, biting and kicking and clawing to get back to where I am now."

Gurney assured Mandarin that he would not blow the whistle on him.

"I sure hope so," said Mandarin. "A guy like you would probably never believe it, but I love this business. It's all I know and ever will know. My world is bounded on the left by the Barrymore Theatre and on the right by the opening number of *Gypsy,* and I'm damned proud of it. I'll sing the entire score of *Bye Bye Birdie* for you, if you like."

"Not just now," Gurney said. "But thanks."

And Gurney, who had considered Mandarin a rather oily type minutes before, left the fellow's office with the feeling that he was quite a touching and even appealing figure.

* * *

Despite the heavy trancelike nature of the project—not a word of the libretto on paper, strangely evasive producers, songs that dealt with Paris and failed love affairs that were designated for a show about violence in a homicide bureau—Gurney was amazed to find that he was quite content with his new career. Going off to work on *Violencia* each morning represented a routine of sorts, and he realized that he enjoyed routines of almost any kind, especially new ones, before they became routine. He had expected to draw even closer to Hartog as a friend. When this did not come about, the director, sensing the younger man's disappointment, put it all on his mother, apologizing on her behalf.

"Essie has finally gotten up the courage to meet you, Paul, and soon we'll all be sitting down for a delicious dinner. In a restaurant, of course. Essie hasn't cooked since we left Vienna."

Gurney had expected to spend more time on a social basis with the show's composer as well, but Norman Welles was standoffish in this area. Gurney guessed that the upscale circles in which Welles mixed would make a former homicide dick feel uncomfortable. So it came as a surprise when one night the composer called him at his apartment, to tell him that he and Tippy had decided to back away from one another and just be friends.

"I suddenly realized that I can't have anything pressing on my mind while I'm doing a show. When you work as hard as I do, you find yourself exhausted, with nothing left to give to someone in the way that only I know how to give when I'm available."

He then said that since Gurney was a young fellow, he probably knew a lot of hot young girls.

"Is there anyone you could fix me up with? You worked in homicide, Paul, and probably met all kinds of low types, which quite frankly are my preference—so long as I don't come away with a dose.

"You see, Paul," he said with a sweet and almost wounded note in his voice, "that way I can have my pleasure and won't have to be seriously involved with anyone, which would distract me from the show."

Gurney found it flattering that the attractive, well-known composer should be asking him for women. But the truth was he couldn't really think of anyone except perhaps the nice one-armed woman who worked at the Bureau and who had been kind enough to sublet the apartment to him at a ridiculously low rent.

"There *is* a girl named Angela you might like," said Gurney.

"Fine. But are you sure she won't give me crabs or some other souvenir like that? Jesus Christ, that's all I'd need."

"Make sure you don't give *her* something," said Gurney, surprising himself with the strength of his reaction.

Welles, at the other end, was silent, sensing the ex-dick's anger and continuing to live in fear of it.

"I'm only teasing, Paul, you know that," he said. "But I've got to be careful and preserve my health for the good of the show and the potential enrichment of us all."

Gurney went ahead and set up the date. His feeling, in the end, was that Welles, in his own way, was a decent and generous person when it came right down to the core. Or close to the core. It might work out nicely for Angela to meet that type of fellow. Then, too, something might develop that would have a happy result for the two of them.

A few nights later, Angela called Gurney and thanked him for arranging the date with Welles. She said she liked him, but that he was awfully rigid about his schedule.

"He kept looking at his watch during dinner, and after an hour he said that was all the time he could spare. And he wants to make a sex date for January twelfth, at three in the afternoon before he meets his accountant. And I'm not even sure he likes me."

Angela was a girl of almost heartbreaking loveliness, but was quite unsure of herself, obviously because of the arm.

"Of course he liked you," said Gurney, feeling queasy and wondering why he had served her up to the composer. "If he didn't, he's in a lot of trouble with me. And don't keep that sex date."

He said good-bye to Angela and realized that she would probably do anything he asked her to. *That settles it,* he thought. *I'm taking Angela to the opening, even though it will probably land me in hot water with my ex-wife.*

On an impulse, Gurney decided one night to pay a visit to his old bureau. He arrived during the night shift, picked up a pass from the desk sergeant, and immediately headed for the office in which he'd worked for eleven years. Nothing much appeared to have changed. He glanced at a dummied-up copy of the latest issue of *The Homicider* and had mixed feelings when he saw that John Gable, his replacement, seemed to have picked up his style, or at least a pale simulation of it. It troubled him that only the most discerning dick would notice that Gurney's distinct personal touch was missing. Or perhaps he was underestimating his old pals, an unfortunate tendency of his.

Standing in the office where he no longer worked, Gurney suddenly felt strange and somewhat unwelcome. As a result, he decided to make it a quick visit. On his way out, he stopped by the office of Detective Turner, his former boss. The gentlemanly pipe smoker was at his desk, working late. He looked up, nodded to Gurney, and continued to study a police report on his desk.

"How's it going, Wally?" said Gurney. "I was in the neighborhood and thought I'd stop by."

"Your show'll probably be a flop," said Turner, barely taking his eyes from the report. "All of them are."

Gurney felt as if a pail of ice water had been poured on his head.

"What about *Fair Lady*?" he fired back.

"You should live so long."

"I'd better get going,"said Gurney. "It's been a nice visit. Maybe I'll come back some other time."

"You do that," said Turner, without enthusiasm.

Gurney walked toward the door, then stopped and decided to make a last-ditch effort to win back the affection of his old boss.

"Would you and the wife like to attend the opening of my new show?"

Turner responded with a look that fell just short of being a sneer.

Gurney took this as his cue to leave. It was obvious that his ex-boss still resented his leaving the Bureau. And Gurney could understand why someone who had devoted his entire life to crimebusting would resent an individual who had traded in a career in homicide for a whirl at show business.

But he also saw that the visit, unlike the farewell dinner in his honor, represented his final good-bye to the Bureau. You can't go home again, after all, he concluded—especially if you are an ex-homicider.

Scene 4

The following night, Clement Hartog called and said that Essie was now anxious to have dinner with Gurney.

"She's ashamed of herself for having put this off for so long."

Gurney and the director met at a small but highly regarded restaurant in Chinatown, with Essie joining them a bit later. She did not appear to be as old as Gurney had imagined, but the director's mother was certainly the tallest woman he had ever seen; the effect, as she entered Ben To's, was that of a Macy's Thanksgiving Day float, drifting onto the premises. As she stopped to check her coat, Gurney tried to hide his astonishment. The perceptive Clement Hartog picked up on his thoughts.

"Relax, Paul," he said, "she's of average height, but she plans to do the Chief's part on stilts and feels it's important to break them in."

He said that the storklike wooden props had been a trademark of Essie's in her golden Vienna days and that she'd performed all of her starring roles while strapped into them. The custom dated back to a time when she had worked in a notorious Hamburg dive that catered to fetishists. One of the customers was a wealthy German industrialist who liked his women on stilts, and Essie had quickly become his favorite.

"Mother was a game gal with a good sense of fun and was willing to put them on and parade around for Gerhardt as long as he paid the price.

"Those stilts put me through school," said Hartog, becoming emotional for a moment.

Pulling himself together, Hartog went on to say that Essie had enjoyed the feel of her stilts, and began to have custom-made pairs of them shipped in from Rangoon. When she started in theatre, she used stilts in her roles. No question, they inhibited her movement on stage, but they lent an eerie Teutonic coloring to the plays in which she appeared, bringing unexpected praise to the writers and directors with whom she worked. It got to the point where she did not feel comfortable unless she was looking down on the other performers from a spindly wooden vantage point.

"If you wanted Essie Hartog," her son said, with fierce pride, "you had to take her, stilts and all."

According to the director, this meant getting the other actors to wear them as well; to refuse meant having to shout lines up at her.

"In those days, Essie was in great demand. Most Viennese producers were happy to go along with her and were thrilled to sign her at any cost. It's my feeling that *Violencia* will profit by having Mother up on them, since the style hasn't been seen much in the States, if at all."

Hartog conceded that Essie's participation in the musical numbers would, because of the obvious limitations on her movement, be limited to a few stylized gestures above the waist.

"But I've never seen *Violencia* as that much of a dancing show," said Hartog.

Gurney had planned to be casual about his meeting with Essie, but when she joined them, he could not help studying her carefully. She was, after all, the star of *Violencia;* so much depended upon her performance. She had a rich, deep voice which pleased him.

Then, too, her movements had an elegance and a certain grandeur that must have been a carryover from the days when she had been feted by the greats of prewar Vienna. It would not influence her performance, of course, but additionally, she had a directness of style that Gurney felt bordered on rudeness and—that in fact, could only be considered bad manners.

Gurney had a thin scar, visible only on close examination, that ran the length of his chin—just below the lip line—and which tended to blink a bit under fluorescent lighting. He was touchy about it, and tried to keep it concealed with suntans.

Soon after Essie Hartog had taken a seat and unstrapped her stilts, she ordered a stiff drink and said: "Pleased to meet you, Scarface."

Gurney thought that perhaps a character in a dream had made the remark. In his wildest imaginings he could not believe that she had actually said this to him. In all his years at the Bureau, not one of the dicks, who were not beyond a well-placed needle here and there, had ever called attention to his slight deformity. When he looked at Clement Hartog for verification of what he had heard, the director seemed to feel pressured.

"I've thought it over, Paul," he said, "and I've decided to give you a small cut of my percentage in the show."

Gurney realized that Essie Hartog had indeed made the outrageous statement; her celebrated son, deeply embarrassed, had cast about for a way to make it up to Gurney and to show that he wanted to separate himself from his mother's tremendous gaffe.

"My deal is fine," said Gurney, who actually didn't know what his deal was. He braced himself for Essie's next outburst.

Leaning back regally, Essie summoned the owner of the restaurant and ordered a rare duck dish that was not on the menu.

"The way I've always had it prepared for me."

The owner seemed puzzled, as though he had never seen her before. Indeed, it seemed that Essie Hartog's grand style, and her assumption that she would be treated like royalty, were totally un-realistic. This was especially true in the States, where, for all of her Viennese triumphs, she was virtually an untested talent. The owner said politely that he would prepare the dish to the best of his ability. As he turned to go, Essie called out, "And it better be hot, panface," accompanying the remark with a raucous theatrical laugh.

Gurney was less shocked by this vulgarism, perhaps because he had been steeled for it. And it had begun to dawn on him that her rude outbursts were perhaps a way of settling into the vernacular of the show. The Homicide Chief, as planned, would be a coarse, rough-and-tumble type of fellow. Gurney now thought he saw clearly that Essie Hartog was such a complete actress that she intended to im-merse herself totally in the character, becoming the outspoken head of Homicide, both on and off the stage.

Then, too, her natural style was probably earthy and flam-boyant. A difficulty was that Gurney, unused to theatrical folk, was not accustomed to this manner, particularly in women.

In any case, this new line of thinking enabled him to relax somewhat and to enjoy his dinner. His sense of ease, in turn, must have spread to his companions; after the appetizer course, Essie Hartog lumbered over to Gurney's side of the table and gave him a sopping-wet kiss on the mouth.

"You're brilliant and a doll," she said, "and you've created a great role for me. I've had dozens offered to me, of course, but yours was the one that forced me out of retirement. When I read it, I saw that I had no choice."

Essie then described the pitched battle she was having with the producers, the actress insisting that they supply her with a matched pair of Merecedes limousines, one to take her to the theatre at night, the other to return her home. Undertag's office had asked her to scale back her demands, at least until the show was received favorably, its success assured, and Essie confirmed as a major star in the United States, and not just prewar Vienna.

"Can you imagine, Paul?" she said. "They want me to make do with a fucking Chevy pickup."

"Perhaps you ought to go along with them," said Clement Hartog. "See if you can get by with one Mercedes, as a demonstration of good faith."

Essie seemed to melt whenever her son spoke; she looked at him with reverence, savoring his every word, and indeed became quite gentle and feminine in style at these times. Since Gurney had similar feelings about the great director, he appreciated this quality in Essie.

"All right, darling," she said to her son, "if you say so."

Before the dinner was over, Gurney had forgotten that first impression of vulgarity and begun to find Essie's company quite pleasant and convivial, if not entirely winning.

When three months had gone by with nothing specific accomplished—not a line on paper—it was Gurney who felt he could not take the pressure any longer and suggested they really try to get some of their ideas down in the form of actual scenes for the libretto. Gurney felt that although they had come down hard on Norman Welles, at least the composer was coming up with songs, however preposterously wide of the mark they were. Then, too, Undertag had repeatedly insisted that his hands were tied, when it came to future planning, until he had something he could actually show to investors.

"I've got money out the kazoo," he said one day, his lips untypically thin and bitter, "but I'll be damned if I'll risk a dime of it on a show unless someone matches me dollar for dollar."

Against this background, Gurney and Hartog sat down one morning with the idea of actually getting down to cases. After the two had agreed on an opening line or two, Gurney giddily took them down while Hartog, grim, scattered, nervous as a kitten, wrung his hands in his lap.

"I just hope we're right and that we're not going off half-cocked."

Gurney felt like a young colt, anxious to test his legs in an open meadow. Hartog was the wily old trainer, reining him in when he got too frisky and issuing warnings about the terrain.

All of the preplanning and seemingly idle chats the two collaborators had had before getting under way now began to pay dividends. The work went easily and swiftly. Along the way, they uncovered several rich bonanzas in the way of numbers, including one they felt could be quite charming, involving a march of young daughters of dicks in the Bureau in which the tikes express their yearnings to be policewomen. Gurney, realizing he might be out of bounds, dummied up a lyric:

> *Even though*
> *We're little girls*
> *With little curls*
> *And fluffy skirts,*
> *We're dying to be dicks*
> *And make arrests*
> *And make a name*
> *In good ole*
> *Hom—i—ciiiide. . . .*

Hartog liked the sound of it and encouraged his partner to show it to Welles.

"Listen," said the composer after he had reviewed Gurney's efforts, "I'll take help anywhere I can get it. You're obviously not a lyricist, Paul, but perhaps by my really tearing it to shreds and re-working it from the start, I might be able to utilize the germ of an idea you have here."

* * *

When Welles returned with the completed song, Gurney was surprised to see that he had changed only one word: "Little curls" had become "diminutive curls," which, frankly, he did not think of as being a genuine improvement.

Hartog was incensed when he learned that the composer hadn't credited Gurney with making a significant contribution to the number.

"It's a dirty shame, Paul," he said.

"That's all right," said Gurney. "I'm just glad I could help. And it's great that the song might actually make it into the show."

Hartog did not specify how long he wanted the first act to be, and yet he seemed concerned about length and would keep hefting the completed pages and saying: "Let me see how much we got."

One morning, the director appeared with a thin, cadaverous-looking man and asked Gurney if he would mind having the fellow sit in on their session for the day.

"He's Lester Daggo," said Hartog, "an out-of-town critic who will be reviewing the show when it opens on the road."

Hartog explained that Daggo liked to be in at the very start of a show, so that when he reviewed it, further down the line, he could take into consideration the early and perhaps feeble first efforts on the production—and how far it had come along since the work began.

"It's all right with me," said Gurney.

He noted that as he worked, the fellow would occasionally slip noiselessly across the carpet and peer over his shoulder, which was discomforting to the young librettist. But since Hartog had okayed the unorthodox procedure, Gurney went along with it and did his best.

In truth, it was not a good day for the team. To Daggo's credit, he said hardly a word and did not weigh in with suggestions—perhaps sensing, correctly, that Gurney would have found this unacceptable.

Only once did the little critic break into speech.

"I wonder if I could have a junior club sandwich with extra mayonnaise, Clement, but only if it's paid for by the producers."

The director ordered one up immediately and picked up the tab himself.

When Daggo had left for the day, Gurney asked Hartog: "How do you think he liked *Violencia*?"

"It's hard to tell. At times I've felt he's loved a show and he's turned around and blown me out of the water. But I believe in working closely with him and taking my chances.

"And incidentally, I wouldn't underestimate the importance of that club sandwich. Daggo is miserably underpaid and—trust me on this—it meant an awful lot to him. Our paying for that measly lunch could yield dividends in the long run."

When the two felt they had an acceptable first-act draft, Hartog, without stopping for a celebration, asked Gurney to come along to a meeting he had set up with Hunt Feur, one of the greats of the film world, who had produced a number of the director's top films. Admittedly, they were considered to be fluffy family fare, but they were handsomely turned out. It was Hartog's idea that if the powerful Feur liked *Violencia,* he would come through with a rich preproduction deal for the film rights that would solve all of the show's financial difficulties and get that side of the project off their minds.

"Undertag's office should be doing this," said Hartog, "but will they get off their ass? Forget it."

Even though Hunt Feur's office was only five blocks away, the moviemaker sent over a limousine to pick them up, with a young up-and-coming starlet inside to keep them company along the way.

Gurney had never been in a limousine before, although he had hitched a few rides in hearses in connection with his work at the Bureau. Feur's operating style made an impression on him. Nonetheless, he was offended when the starlet turned her back to him and began to nuzzle the director's neck and to put her hand between his legs. Clearly, she was there to entertain only Hartog. The ride was so short it was hardly worth quibbling about. All the same, the rudeness annoyed Gurney, who felt that simple courtesy should have dictated that she put her hand between his legs as well.

Hartog took both the limousine and the young girl—who was virtually panting for a role in one of his pictures—in his stride, a quality Gurney admired in the great director. A simple and modest man, he seemed uninvolved in the glitter and false trappings of the theatrical and film worlds. Either that, or he had never taken advantage of the perks and did not know how to get started at this late date.

Though Feur had gone out of his way to make their short trip almost ridiculously comfortable, he did a mysterious turnabout when the team arrived at his office. The two of them were kept cooling their heels for close to an hour.

"I don't know why I put up with this," said Hartog, who was breathing heavily and trying to control his anger.

Indeed, Gurney did not see why he did either, and felt indignant, not personally, but on behalf of the director.

Feur finally ushered them into his palatial office, embracing Hartog, whom he referred to as "Putzi," and inquiring about Essie Hartog's health. Gurney gathered that the pair had not only been associated in films, but were great pals in Vienna when both were young men, totally unknown but consumed with ambition.

Feur was a pudgy, round-shouldered man of medium height. He was spectacularly bald. Gurney took an immediate dislike to him when the moviemaker, after shaking hands, slapped a cheap cigarillo out of Gurney's mouth and stuffed a cigar of his own into it, saying: "As long as you're smoking, have a *good* one."

The cigar he had forced on Gurney was a grand specimen—long, rich, and fragrant, probably smuggled in from Havana; nonetheless, he thought Feur was out of line in his manner of presenting it. He considered letting the film great know exactly how he felt about this, but decided to hold his temper.

"The one I was smoking was just fine," he said, hardly a rapier-like rejoinder but one he felt would serve for the moment.

A thin and lovely young woman appeared then with a tray of sandwiches. Her eyes were large and startling, her features classically sculpted.

Feur introduced her as Carmela.

"She is my mistress and fahhkkks exquisitely, like an obedient little bunny rabbit."

"A marvelous cook, too," he said, leaning over to take a tweak at her trim fashion model–style buttocks.

Gurney felt sorry for the woman, who indeed seemed forlorn and pathetic. Yet such were the mysteries of attraction that, for all he knew, she may have thrived on the filmmaker's coarse, somewhat vulgar treatment of her.

The trio dug into the sandwiches, Feur eating his behind a huge, magisterial desk. Gurney noticed that the first act draft of *Violencia,* sent on ahead by Hartog, was on prominent display before the producer. He had to admit to himself that it was exciting to see it there.

"Now tell me," said Feur, picking up the script with two fingers and getting egg salad on it, "why the fahhkk do you want to waste your time on this shit, Putzi?"

Not waiting for Hartog to respond, he flung it over his shoulder.

When Gurney saw the pages scattered all over the floor, streaked with egg salad, it was all he could do to keep from punching out Feur. The filmmaker, seemingly out of shape, would have been easy to handle. But he held himself in check, thinking that perhaps this was Feur's way of opening a negotiation, feigning disinterest so as to purchase the material at a ridiculously low price. As though to confirm this notion, Hartog seemed to take Feur's reaction with nonchalance, calmly eating his liverwurst sandwich and not even bothering to meet the producer's eyes.

"What makes you think it's shit?" he asked neutrally.

"Putzi darling, it's shit. Don't I know shit when I see it?

"You want to do scripts?" he said, shoving a stack of them over to Hartog. "Here's scripts. Good stuff, for the whole family. You want to ruin your career, I can't help you."

Gurney saw that Feur had not been fencing at all. He had no confidence whatever in *Violencia*.

"I just can't agree with you, Hunt," said Hartog, wiping his mouth with a napkin and getting up to leave. "And I think we're going to prove that you're dead wrong."

Expecting Hartog to be furious, Gurney was amazed at the director's great control and lack of passion. Was it possible he didn't want to anger Hunt Feur in case *Violencia* was indeed a turkey, forcing the director to crawl back to the producer, hat in hand, begging for the chance to do some more light family fare?

"All right, all right, Putzi," said Feur, conciliatory now. "Go and be a naughty boy. I can never be angry with you, my darling."

With that, he snapped his fingers and an assistant rolled out a giant package on wheels. Carmela followed, holding a cute little purebred puppy which she presented to Clement Hartog.

"Take them both," said Feur, "and I'll see you when you return to your senses."

"And you?" he said to Gurney at the door. "You get nothing."

Gurney realized then that the producer resented him for weaning Clement Hartog away from him. It seemed absurd that Feur would consider an unknown and inexperienced librettist a competitor, but Gurney was now convinced he had the key to Feur's excessively nasty behavior toward him. The great director said good-bye to Feur, then gathered up his puppy and began to wheel the massive package out the door. Gurney was angered by the spectacle—but he also felt a degree of admiration for Feur and his naked use of power. He stopped at the door and addressed the producer.

"I lead a simple life, sir, filled with simple pleasures—but I enjoy every second of it, and millions wouldn't change my way of doing things. People like you can't understand that."

Gurney was curious to see how Feur would respond to this declaration. Was it possible that the display of boldness would result in the filmmaker's suddenly changing his mind and becoming filled with admiration for him? Perhaps Gurney would get a puppy, too.

"Good for you, darling," said Feur, failing to pick up the bait and slamming the door in his face.

In the hallway, while waiting for the elevator, Hartog could not resist peeking into the package. Looking over his shoulder, Gurney saw that it was a brand new electric dryer with high-tech controls. To the best of his knowledge, no other dryer had them.

The gifts were unquestionably generous. Still, Gurney thought he knew how the director must have felt about the rejection of *Violencia*. He put an arm around the older man's shoulder.

"Don't feel bad, Putzi, we'll see it through."

Hartog drew back in anger when he heard the nickname, and Gurney realized it was reserved for those who were part of the director's circle in the early Vienna days. He promised himself he would be careful and never call Hartog "Putzi" again.

"I don't feel that bad about *Violencia*," said Hartog. "I know how good it is. What bothers me is that I'm in his debt now, because of the goddamned dryer and this cute little puppy. If I had any guts, I'd give both of them back, but I can't because I love them too much."

He shook his head, half in admiration.

"The sonofabitch always knew how to get around me."

*   *   *

The next morning, Hartog conceded he had made a huge blunder in showing the half-completed libretto to Hunt Feur and he began to flagellate himself for his error. At the very minimum, he felt, he should have had the filmmaker travel to see *him;* he believed it might have made a world of difference.

"Why do I degrade myself so?" he asked rhetorically. "When will it sink in that it's a mistake to run like an errand boy whenever someone whistles?"

Hartog then went over the line of self-pity into actual bitter tears. Gurney, while consoling his friend, had to observe that for a man of his stature, the celebrated director had surprising chinks in his self-confidence.

Hartog finally pulled himself together. With great gentleness, he took Gurney's arm—they were always taking each other by the arm—and said: "Do you think we might continue?"

The two pushed on, and, as Hartog had promised, the second act, much shorter than the first by traditional design, did indeed take care of itself. In its overall scheme, it involved a brutal song-and-dance grilling sequence in which the captured black dick is tricked into confessing that he did indeed murder a series of innocent pants-pressers; the continuing struggle between the Homicide Chief and his detective son over whether to simply beat the suspect's ass to a pulp or to handle him with socially enlightened methods; and a payoff scene in which the Homicide Chief wearily cleans out his desk and drives off in his squad, while his forward-looking detective son, who is to take over the department, screams after him in tears born of love and hate that he is a fine man and a good dick in many ways but that his methods are old-hat.

The two collaborators decided that a "Hookers' Dance" and a "Mad Dog Shooting" ballet were possible second-act production numbers; mild comic relief might be supplied by a song in which the young detective hero's girlfriend petulantly complains that he wears his gun at all times—at weddings, at dances, in steam baths, and even, by inference, when he goes to bed with her. The musical lament, slyly, would be called, "I Can't Get His Gun Off."

Another comedy selection, and a possible show-stopping sleeper if Norman Welles came through on the lyrics, would be called "Let Us Inform You of Your Constitutional Rights," to be sung by a quartet of rookie dicks as they comedically practice quite the reverse on an elderly suspect, slamming down the door of his apartment, grabbing his favorite sister's ass, pissing on his personal belongings, and finally hauling him down to headquarters, where they shove his head into a toilet bowl that they continually flush until, bleeding, pissed on, and thoroughly humiliated, the suspect is ready to confess that he's killed the Pope if they want him to.

The libretto took a mere two weeks to complete and probably could have been wrapped up in one had not Gurney dragged his feet a bit, reluctant to end this satisfying phase of his work. He knew that once rehearsals got under way, Hartog would begin to function solely as a director. As a result, there would be little time for those wonderful delicatessen snacks and the exchange of anecdotes, Hartog holding forth on movie greats, Gurney pitching in with unusual moments along the homicide beat. Indeed, when Gurney handed over the final page, there was a sadness in the room. Gurney, whose work at Homicide had taught him to conceal, if not eliminate, his feelings, merely tightened his jaw and looked stoically out the window. Hartog, a man of the theatre and consequently unafraid of revealing emotion, wept openly for a moment, and was not ashamed of his tears.

The director suggested that they celebrate the completion of the first draft of *Violencia* by passing up their regular snack and going out for drinks and a more sumptuous lunch at a nearby restaurant, one frequented by theatre regulars.

The waiter who took their order appeared to have inside information on the show.

"I hear it's very Jewish," said the man.

Gurney quickly corrected him, wondering at the same time how that strange notion had gotten currency.

A famed theatrical producer, known for his acerbic wit, strolled by and said to Hartog: "Sounds like you've got a million-dollar baby. I just hope it doesn't die in the cradle."

And then he strolled off to his own table.

Hartog's face was flushed with rage. He kept getting up from his seat, then sitting down and glaring at the producer.

"I wish I could take him on. But he'd only cut me to pieces. I just don't have the verbal skills to cope with him."

Gurney felt that in some remote way Hartog was telling him to challenge the producer on his behalf—since the ex-homicider was allegedly the verbal one—but Gurney could think of no withering rejoinders at the moment; added to which, he had not really felt insulted by the man.

A noted columnist came by then and whipped out his pad, as if waiting for Hartog to come up with a few anecdotes. Hartog made a few fumbling tries, but they came to nothing and the man finally put away his pencil and pad with a smirk.

"I can never think of anything to tell that man," said the director. "It's probably held back my career, too, since other directors always have a fund of stories ready to pour out on the spot. Imagine how much it would have helped *Violencia* if I'd had a few juicy tidbits to tell him. But my mind as usual went blank."

Gurney saw this as another attractive example of Hartog's self-effacing manner; but he had to admit it would have been fun to read about *Violencia* and see his own name in the widely read Broadway column.

Undertag came over then and congratulated them on the completion of the script. True to his style of only investing when there was someone else in the picture to match him dollar for dollar, he picked up half of the lunch tab.

Scene 5

S everal days later, Undertag summoned the three collaborators to his office and said that he had read *Violencia* and felt it wasn't bad at all, although it could probably profit by having risque jokes peppered throughout the show for surefire laughs.

"And you could write them, too, you sonofabitch," he said, poking Gurney in the ribs, "if only you wouldn't hold out on us."

Gurney did not know where the producer had gotten this notion and he wasn't sure if he should be flattered or insulted by the remark. In any event, Undertag said that he had shown the script to the movie companies and there wasn't a shred of interest from any of them—which killed off Hollywood as a source of investment funds. Additionally, the record companies, which traditionally backed musical shows, had been burned badly in recent years by flop musicals, many of them turkeys produced by Undertag. Understandably, they weren't too anxious to toss in any money either. There was one music group, however, a newcomer to the field, that had expressed some interest in the detectivey musical.

"Would you fellows consider auditioning the show for the kid in charge? He's got money coming out the kazoo."

Welles and Hartog said they would just as soon not—but that under the circumstances they would go along.

When they were alone, Hartog told Gurney: "I shouldn't be doing this. They ought to invest simply on the basis of my past performance. Auditioning for some young snotnose is definitely the wrong thing for me to do. And yet here I am again, doing it. When the hell am I ever going to learn?"

Gurney, of course, had nothing to lose, since the ball would have to be carried by Clement Hartog, who would act out scenes from the libretto, and Norman Welles, who would come in on the songs, accompanied by Tito Passionato.

The audition was held in Undertag's office. Also present were Toileau, Mandarin, Miss Hottle, Tippy, and several blueblooded friends of Norman Welles who were there as "clackers," their function being to hoot and holler and laugh and cry, particularly in response to the songs, and to create a general atmosphere of enthusiasm.

Toileau, dignified, immaculately barbered, served as host of the proceedings, offering drinks to the assemblage. He introduced the collaborators to the record company head, a young tycoon named Jabby Baranoff, who had made a fortune as a rock guitarist, then eventually taken over the company that produced his records. Baranoff, a bearded and scrappy little bundle of a man, had gotten his major break in a curious manner. One night, early in his career, while on his way to a rock concert engagement, his hands had become mangled in a car door accident. Instead of canceling, Baranoff had taken a bold step: Virtually fainting from the pain, he'd crawled up to the stage and proceeded to snatch at the guitar strings with his teeth, gnawing and sucking at them; the result was a bloody, slobbering, chaotic sound that had pleased the assembled youngsters and started the musician on the road to millions.

Hartog sketched in a rough overview of the show. Then, with some fervor, he acted out several of the scenes for Baranoff, stopping so that Welles could fill in the song numbers. The sight of the great director performing for some pipsqueak—who could not have been more than twenty-five—was not a cheering one for Gurney. He saw, however, that there was probably no other course to take and, once again, he admired Hartog's courage and humility. There was a lesson in all of this for Gurney, though he wasn't entirely sure what it was.

Welles was much more dramatic in this recital of the scenes. In putting across the light love tunes, Gurney felt, the composer was guilty of overacting, contorting his face and singing with animal passion, only inches from the record company executive's hairy face.

This did not seem to bother Baranoff, however; the young tycoon laughed without control at all the right places, wept when it was in order, and, in short, reacted exactly as the collaborators, in their dreams, might have wanted. This gave great heart to Clement Hartog, who built up momentum as he neared the climactic scene of *Violencia*. Finally, he plunged headlong into it, his delivery bringing Baranoff to his feet, laughing, crying, and applauding all at once.

"Wait a minute while I catch my breath," he said, appearing to be more emotionally drained than the hardworking Hartog. "What can I say! I love it. I love it more than my own schvonce. You've got an authentic pisser of a show here and of course I want in."

"For how much?" Undertag asked, virtually rubbing his hands in anticipation.

Gurney, for one, was delighted at the producer's businesslike directness.

"Just let me get back to my office for a look at the books," said Baranoff. "That's all I ask."

When the music executive had left, there was much speculation in the room as to how much money his company would invest in the musical. Undertag guessed somewhere around two hundred thousand, in which case he would match the amount—and the show would be more or less financed.

"It's probably a stupid move on my part," said Undertag, "considering the long gray line of stinkers I've backed. But if the kid is crazy enough to come in, I'll jump in with him."

When Baranoff called some twenty minutes later, Undertag ceremoniously transferred him to the speakerphone so that his voice could be heard throughout the room.

"Just got in this second, and true to my word I'm calling. Bottom line, I'm not investing a nickel in the show. But I couldn't say it right there, right to your face. I had to wait till I got back to the safety of my own office, where I don't have to meet your eyes. Did I like it? Sure, although most of my reactions were playacting and I didn't care for it one-tenth as much as I pretended. The trouble is, I can't express my feelings to anyone who's standing right in front of me. I admit it's a problem, although you'll have to admit it hasn't held back my career. Am I dealing with it? You bet your ass. Four sessions a week, on the couch and on my back. I wish I could say I'd seen some daylight. Meanwhile, I'm sorry if my behavior has caused you grief."

"Sure, fella," said Undertag with a little smirk, and hung up. "This show has been one big pain in the ass since I took it on."

"What have you taken on?" asked Hartog in a flash of anger, the first time he had lashed out so directly at the producer of *Violencia*. "What have you done? Not a fucking thing."

"Easy now," said Undertag, who seemed frightened by the unexpected outburst. "Whatever the outcome, I don't want to lose you as a personal friend, Clement. You know how much I love Essie and how strongly I feel your mom will tear the roof off the theatre if we're lucky enough to get that far."

"For Christ's sakes," said Welles, scowling bitterly, "I could finance the show myself if only some of my wealthy friends were in the country and not vacationing in Montecatini."

The remark was hollow. Gurney saw through it. It meant nothing.

"All right," said Hartog, getting to his feet and dismissing Undertag with a wave, "you're the producer—produce. And don't bother me with the details."

It was thrilling for Gurney to see the director finally behave with some arrogance. It had some effect on Undertag, too.

"Okay," he said, pale and somewhat shaken. "I just don't want you going around this city and Hollywood, bad-mouthing me and not being my friend."

Several days later, Undertag summoned the collaborators and said he hated to ask, but would they do one more audition, this time for the theatre party ladies.

"If they like *Violencia* and put it on their subscription lists, we can count on a strong advance sale—and be well on the way to a production."

Hartog was not at all pleased by this suggestion, but once again, begrudgingly, he said that he would go along.

For some unfathomable reason, both he and Welles, this time around, were at the top of their game. As a result, when Hartog orated the scenes and Welles performed his songs, Gurney, for the first time, caught a hint of what the show might be. There was a genuine smell of violence and homicide about it, all of it having an authentic gun-metal gray feel to it. Throughout the modest little audition, Gurney thought he heard the wail of squad car sirens, the hum of excitement in the bullpen when a fresh homicide is posted on the bulletin board, the dull, thick weight of bone-bangers coming down on a perpetrator's head. It all came back to him . . . the fear in a suspect's eyes during the most routine of investigations, the look of vengeance through the bars from a hood who's been given a stiff sentence, the red-streaked demented condition of a room in which there's been a stabbing, particularly if it has involved jealous lovers.

Strangely enough, Welles' light romantic songs of Paris and

young love, far from being a distraction, served to give the show
an ironic counterpoint, making the other scenes all the more glum
and deadly. Gurney felt new respect for the composer and began
to understand what he was trying to achieve. Gurney listened as
though in a spell, broken only momentarily during the "Mad Dog
Shooting" ballet sequence when one of the theatre party ladies
whispered to a companion:

"It's just like what goes on in my apartment."

Gurney began to feel a drumbeat of excitement over the
show's potential, and was not overly concerned about the ladies'
reaction, which, predictably, was tepid. After some perfunctory
applause, they filed out, for the most part without comment. A stout
middle-aged woman stopped for a moment to address Gurney.

"Of course, I'm not going to book *Violencia,* there are too
many things around that are good this season. But would you do
one service to yourselves and to the American theatre?"

"What's that?" asked Gurney.

"Listen to Mr. Toileau, and lose 'doody.'"

When the ladies had left, Undertag announced that, unfortunately, the audition had not worked out as planned.

"None of the broads are willing to book the show. The only
group that showed any interest was an organization that's trying to
cure hammertoes."

"How many members do they have?" asked Welles.

"Not enough," said Undertag.

"That's your concern," Hartog said grandly, putting on a
black cape that Gurney had never seen him wear before. "I've conducted my last audition. Paul and I have work to do."

When they were in the street, and Welles had gone off to get a quick
suntan at a nearby gym—he belonged to gyms all over the city—
Gurney asked the director what he had meant by his last remark.

"I thought we were all finished."

Hartog said yes, they were, in a sense, but while they waited for the financing to kick in, they might as well try a nip here and a tuck there.

"There's no end to the improvements you can make."

Gurney felt a little sick at the thought of going back to chew on the same bone. He told the director that frankly he had no heart to do so.

"There's no money, no theatre," he said, detecting a grain of self-pity in his tone, "and even though I'm new in this field and have no credits, I've got to feel that I'm working toward a real goal."

Hartog said he understood and suggested that they tinker with the show at Blandishments, the country estate to which he and Essie often repaired when they needed to escape the madness of the city. But Hartog admitted that quite frankly, although the property had rolling acres and waterfalls and no end of comforts, it was all a fraud in one sense, since he was unable to relax even there.

"I'm only happy when I've got my teeth in a show."

The director then suggested that Gurney might feel better about the trip if he brought someone along.

"If it's a woman, however, I'm afraid you won't be able to sleep over with her. Essie just won't allow it. Even though she worked in waterfront dives for much of her life, she's prudish about such arrangements."

Gurney said the issue was academic.

"I'm going it alone these days and have no one to bring."

The next morning, however, before he set out for Blandishments in his squad, he thought of the lovely though one-armed Angela from whom he had leased his charming apartment. He was a little nervous about dialing her number, sensing a possible rejection, but to his delight—and with no coy hesitation—she accepted the invitation.

"I'd love to come," she said, almost as if she'd been waiting months for such a call.

Driving up to Blandishments, Gurney leaned over from time to time to give Angela a friendly hug, but for the most part spent the time appraising her as a future and perhaps permanent partner. Unlike his ex-wife's shrill voice, Angela's was deep and sensual; as though to compensate for her handicap, her other parts were extraordinary—her bosom full-blown, her waist slim, and her legs young, restless, enthusiastic, and most desirable. But the arm, of course, was always in the picture. Though Gurney felt he could handle it with little difficulty, he was, to be honest with himself, worried about what others would think when he showed up with her at parties.

Nothing ever comes easy to me, he thought. *In order to get a delightful and exquisite young girl, intelligent and easy on the nerves, I have to take one with an arm missing.*

Blandishments was all that Hartog had promised, a natural paradise of rich, exotic shrubbery, mysteriously gladed brooks, and delightful little paths and bridges. The interior of the house was messy, however, the tables and chairs sticky and full of crumbs from meals eaten days before. The director was there to greet them, but although his chest was bare and his dress rustic and countrified—Bermuda shorts and open-toed moccasins—he looked exactly as he did in the city: grim, graying, and totally preoccupied.

"It's no use," he said. "With all this luxury—and I'd hate to tell you what it costs me a month—I still can't relax."

Essie appeared then, carrying Feur's gift dog in her arms, the pup all dressed up as a small child in a sailor suit. It was the first time Gurney had seen the great Viennese actress without her stilts. Although Hartog had been charming to Angela, his mother completely ignored her; taking Gurney aside, she said that she had heard about his divorce and that her heart broke each time she thought about it. She took his head into her bosom and held it there, appearing to be deeply troubled and sympathetic about Gurney's marital difficulties. Still, Gurney resented Essie's cold treatment of his friend.

"Angela's a terrific kid," he said, removing his head from the actress's bosom.

Whether Essie approved or not, Gurney felt that Angela was his guest, his choice, and that the Hartogs could either accept this or he would be forced to leave. If he and Angela stormed out, it would probably not end the collaboration, but it certainly wouldn't shore it up.

Essie explained that the reason she refused to allow Angela and Gurney to stay over was that Gertie, as she'd named Hunt Feur's gift dog, would probably realize they were sleeping together.

"What if you change your mind and go back to your wife, Paul? It would totally confuse little Gertie and complicate future relations between all of us."

Gurney realized that in a very short time, Essie had begun to conceive of the small thoroughbred puppy as the second child she'd never been able to have.

Hartog and Gurney took a stab at some scenes, but it soon became clear that they were not going to be able to get much done in the easygoing atmosphere of Blandishments. The day was spent in a relaxed manner, the director giving his visitors complete tours of the house and grounds that were quite frankly more thoroughgoing than Gurney would have wanted.

After a surprisingly uninspired dinner—small portions of hamburger, sliced bread, and coleslaw—Essie Hartog suggested they all have a nude swim in one of the secluded brooks, which, she said, was lighted artificially in such a way that a dull glaze hung in the air, making it impossible for them to get clinical looks at one another.

"Sounds good to me," said Gurney, although, actually, it did not. Clement Hartog would get an unimpeded look at Angela's almost flawless body, which had to be considered a treat, even in the uncertain light. All that was in it for Gurney was the possibility of seeing the venerable Essie Hartog in the nude. Even though the aging actress had a remarkably well-preserved and stately figure, with high, torpedoing breasts, Gurney, perhaps swinishly, did not contemplate the experience with any pleasure. The thought of Clement Hartog in the nude was equally uninspiring.

At the edge of the brook, Angela was the first to disrobe, and did not so much take off her clothes as fling them aside with abandon; Gurney's thought was that either she had gone for countless nude swims, or that she was eager to please him and would do anything at all to do so. In the yellowing, faded light of the brook, the swim became more of a tentative dance than anything else, all of them gliding along like small ships, aware of one another's presence, tensely nonchalant about it. When they'd had enough of the water, Essie announced that she had changed her mind and that Angela and Gurney could indeed stay over and sleep in the same room.

"I don't know what possessed me to think otherwise," said Essie.

It was as if they had passed an examination.

They were given a large, cheery room with a roaring fireplace. The fire seemed to have a sensuous effect on Angela. She removed her clothing slowly this time, moving her body in rhythm to the flames as if they were dancing partners. Gurney almost fainted with pleasure at the sight. Every few minutes, Clement Hartog opened the door, took a quick look in, and shouted out, "Good night, Angela and Paul," with a certain petulance. It was as if he wanted to make sure they went right to sleep and did not have sex in his guest room. After his appearances had tapered off—and then stopped—Angela hopped into bed with Gurney, and what they did for a while was to snuggle, using each other as blankets in the chill air. Gurney could not recall ever being happier. The key to the way in which Angela made love was gratitude. She was completely delighted each time he kissed and touched her body, as if she were a small girl receiving an endless cascade of holiday presents. This was entirely new territory for Gurney. Only once did she become annoyed—when he kissed her several times on what he thought of as her unfortunate side to show her it was all right and he didn't mind.

"That really isn't necessary," she said, sitting up in bed for a moment.

But then she pressed her lovely body against his once again, making him wonder why he didn't change the direction of his life at that very moment and try to snap her up forever. It was probably the arm, he guessed.

Hartog and Gurney were the first to awaken the next morning; they ate a light breakfast, strolled about the grounds, and, for the first time since Gurney had arrived, talked about *Violencia*.

"I would be willing to work on the show indefinitely," said the director. "That's how much I believe in the material. Let Undertag get his financing two years from now if that's the best he can do. Meanwhile, we keep refining the libretto and helping Norman with his songs. How's that for a plan?"

Strolling through the massive estate, Gurney suddenly became annoyed with the director, though he'd never felt that way before. Hartog owned all of this acreage. It was true he couldn't relax and enjoy it, but he did have it. And with his great fortune, he could easily afford to work for as long as he liked without reward.

But what about Gurney, an ex-homicider with an uncertain future and hardly a pittance salted away.

"I just can't continue this way, Clement," he said. "Sooner or later, I'm going to have to figure out a way to earn a few dollars."

"Well, I suppose I can see your point," said Hartog. "I can't lend you any money, if that's what you're getting at, since that's the one thing I never do."

"I don't want any of your money," said Gurney, this time having difficulty keeping his anger in check. Maybe it was because he really did expect Hartog to write out a check for him—and the director had guessed his thoughts.

Hartog then said he recognized that from all appearances he was comfortable and could afford to breeze along while waiting for *Violencia* to fall into place.

"My situation is not as good as it looks, however. Blandishments is tremendously expensive to maintain. And then there's Essie to take care of. Her acting and vocal and dance lessons alone cost more than most people earn in six months. Just the other day, she mentionned fencing instructions. And, of course, now there's Gertie the dog to take care of. You've only got to look after yourself, Paul. In many ways, you're in much better shape than I am."

"Now listen," said Gurney, frustrated at not being able to show as much anger as he wanted to, "there's just no comparison."

"I supposed you're right," said Hartog. "And I can also see for the first time that I'm the only one around here who believes passionately in *Violencia*."

"Wrong," said Gurney. "I believe in it, too . . . as much as you and maybe more. I just can't go on this way forever."

Scene 6

Gurney finally made it clear to Clement Hartog that in order to push on, he needed the assurance of a Broadway production. Work was then broken off while Undertag presumably went about trying to drum up financing for the project, avoiding at all costs spending a nickel of his own unless it was matched by someone else's money.

Gurney felt glum about *Violencia,* in part because there was a chance that all the months he had invested in the show had come to nothing—and perhaps more because he missed the daily sessions with Clement Hartog. He did not see the director for a week and had the unhappy feeling that the theatre maestro was huddled with another fellow on a fresh family-oriented project that would prove to be easier sledding than the thorny homicide musical. Out of pride, he avoided calling Hartog. He took Angela to dinner a few times and was surprised to find himself slithering into restaurants and taking inconspicuous tables. The arm did not play a part, in this case. It was rather as if he were still married and trying to avoid his wife.

He enjoyed being with Angela, who regarded him worshipfully and showed great appreciation when he treated her to expensive dinners. The combination of her great-eyed shyness and approval gave him considerable confidence. Untypically, he found himself ordering headwaiters about and generally putting service people through their paces.

He made love to her at first with great care, as though in deference to her problem. But she made it clear quickly that she preferred to be jostled about and could take care of herself.

"Can you be a little rougher?" was her only instruction to him. There were times when he made love to her all night long, and with a certain desperation—as if she had been given to him on loan and at some point would have to be returned. He had never had a woman turn herself over to him so completely—body and, as far as he could tell, soul. He felt it must have been some kind of happy accident. And yet, with some irony, he was uncomfortable only when she took her time leaving in the morning. It was as if she were waiting around for the ultimate gift: getting to stay around indefinitely— even though legally it was her own apartment.

To maintain a kind of tie with *Violencia,* he called not Hartog but Norman Welles for dinner one night. Gurney took Angela along and the composer turned up with Tippy. The four returned to Lumpy's, the colorful hangout within a stone's throw from Gurney's old bureau.

During dinner, the composer showed his usual surprising flashes of generosity and good nature. When Gurney's duck was served to him overcooked, Welles said, "Here, take this, Paul," tossing half of his own portion on the ex-dick's plate. "I want you to have it, even though I'm starving and could easily eat the whole thing."

Gurney, of course, was touched by the gesture.

Welles seemed not a bit disturbed by the uncertainty surrounding the *Violencia* production, although perhaps he was, and was trying to cover up his fears.

"Just as soon as the show is on," he said, "you and I will go to Acapulco, Paul, either in triumph or disgrace."

When the two women had gone off to the powder room, Welles said he found Angela to be a sweet and wonderful person.

"Tippy is, too," said Gurney.

"And so is your ex-wife."

"When did you meet her?" said Gurney, who could not recall introducing her to the composer.

"Oh, I just called her up one day," said Welles, "and we had a wonderful talk on the phone."

This seemed peculiar to Gurney; he wondered if perhaps Welles hadn't followed up the chat by driving to his old house on Staten Island and fucking her brains out. Oddly enough, Gurney was not overly concerned about this possibility—a sure sign that he may have been emotionally free of his ex-wife. And besides, he knew something about Welles' habits. At best, the composer had allotted her only a brief, carefully parceled out period of time in bed, which would not have pleased the difficult Gilda Gurney.

The dinner was a drowsy, comfortable one, topped off by free brandies sent over by the owner, and finally by a visit from Lumpy himself, a wizened ex-dick who had been all over the world and spent much time on the China coast. Lumpy regaled them with anecdotes, building up to his favorite, one that Gurney had often heard before, in which the saloon owner was taken into custody by the shore police for being caught masturbating at midnight in Hong Kong Harbor.

"I love it," said Norman Welles, almost before he'd heard the punch line. " God, you're colorful."

Gurney was willing to stay on at Lumpy's all night, and had a feeling the two women felt the same way. But Welles, who had rigid sleeping patterns, suggested they start back.

Outside Lumpy's, in the pale homicidal light, Kicker was waiting for them. Huge, shambling, wearing a black stocking hat and a torn pea jacket, the foot-fighter shoved Gurney and then danced back a few steps.

"It's me and you tonight, Gurns. We've had this date for too long. I think you're Broadway and you're shit."

Gurney could not find Kicker's eyes and realized that the fabled foot-fighter, untypically, had been drinking heavily. As the two circled one another, Gurney, who had been badly shaken by the suddenness of the challenge, found that he'd become unnaturally calm. For all of his size and power, Kicker was not that much of a threat once you knew his fighting style. He would pick his moment and deliver his best kick; if it failed to make contact, he was, at least for the moment, an easy target.

Most of the homicide dicks at some point or another had taken him on; Gurney could think of only one who had been injured by Kicker: a certain Detective Tuttweiler who had been writing a novel and, as a result, was distracted during the encounter. Fighting Kicker was virtually a Bureau tradition, so much so that no dick would ever think of filing arrest charges against the street fighter. Still, there was always the possibility that Kicker had been taking classes in advanced foot-fighting and had refined his style—so that a wild kick might actually land with devastating force.

As the two circled one another, Angela became frightened and asked Lumpy, who had come out to watch the proceedings, if he would stop them. Tippy, on the other hand, looked on with fascination, shouting out: "Let them fight."

At a point when Kicker seemed ready to let one fly, Welles, surprisingly, and with great courage, stepped between the two antagonists.

"Leave this man alone," he said to Kicker in the manner of an angry schoolteacher. "For Christ's sakes, we're collaborating on a musical comedy."

Gurney thanked the composer and eased him aside, keeping a wary eye on Kicker, who, somewhat predictably, seized the moment to let his great size 14 fly. Gurney was prepared for the kick, easily parried it, and timed a punch with great precision to Kicker's

kidneys. When the hood dropped to his knees, Gurney caught himself doing a self-congratulatory boxing ring shuffle, and was then
embarrassed about it.

"That's all you know is gut-punching," said the fallen
Kicker. "Is that what they teach you on Broadway?"

"You've got the gut for it, Kicker," said Gurney.

Lumpy helped Kicker to his feet and gave Gurney a funny
look, as though he had done something out of line. A few homicide
dicks had come out to watch the brief fight, and they, too, appeared
to be disgusted with Gurney and allied in this case with the once-
scorned foot-fighter.

Angela, Tippy, and Norman Welles, in a show of solidarity, gathered round Gurney and dusted him off. The four then drove
off in Norman Welles' sleek Italian sports sedan.

"I should be in bed by now," said the composer, who seemed
revved up by the brief street brawl, "but I'm too excited to go home.
Let's stop and have a brandy."

At a late-night bar, the four sat around and reviewed the
fight, treating Gurney as if he were a hero. He enjoyed all the fuss,
but it troubled him that Lumpy and the dicks had lined up on Kicker's
side. And the remarks about Broadway plagued him for days.

After a week had passed, and it seemed that *Violencia* had gone down
the drain, Norman Welles, of all people, came through with a strange
first-time theatre angel who guaranteed three hundred thousand
dollars in backing for the Broadway-bound musical. It struck Gurney
as ironically apt that Welles, with all of his bluff and bluster, and
whom no one had taken seriously, should have been the one to save
the day.

It was Undertag who called Gurney and told him about their
savior, a certain Hal Carioca, known in financial circles as a mysterious wheeler-dealer with a reputation for successfully getting in and

out of slippery business ventures. Carioca's most widely known coup had been the merchandising of a salad oil which could also be used as a greaseless hair dressing, when there was a little left. The product had been a disaster in the States, but Carioca had seen enormous possibilities for the dressing in the dollar-starved countries of Central and South America. Taking over the reins of the shaky little salad oil company, he quickly turned it into a fortune-producing colossus and then got out quickly when tests began to show that even modest applications of the dressing resulted in extensive hair loss.

Undertag said that there were no apparent strings attached to Carioca's involvement in *Violencia*. The story was almost too good to be believed. Welles had simply run into Carioca at a Junior League charity ball. He was a man who evidently operated on hunches, and had quickly warmed to the risky crapshooting nature of the investment; and, of course, there was the possibility of astronomically high returns if *Violencia* were to come in as a hit. What made him ideal as a backer, according to Undertag, was that he had no pretensions about knowing the business and no suggestions to make—apart from a possible fraternity hijinks panty-raid number, which the producer had quickly knocked down as being inappropriate.

"He feels that we're the experts and is leaving it all to us," said Undertag.

It struck Gurney that Carioca might well have had cause to doubt the producer, considering Undertag's virtually unbroken record of stage disasters.

Undertag said that Carioca had delivered him a check for the three hundred thousand and that Welles and Hartog were at the office, preparing to have a drink in celebration of the news.

"Why don't you join us, Paul. And if there's a girl you're boffing, bring her, too."

Gurney had been flattered by the personal call from the producer, but he felt the last remark was not only antiquated but rude, taking too much for granted about the degree of friendship between them. Gurney had never said a word to Undertag about his private life. For all the producer knew—unless someone else had sketched in the details—Gurney might have been happily married, with a couple of kids, and living in the suburbs. If such were the case, the "boffing" remark would have been gross, indeed.

Nontheless, Gurney hailed a cab and got the driver to race down to Undertag's office.

Clement Hartog, smoking hungrily, was the first to greet him.

"This project certainly has had its ups and downs. Never seen one like it."

Gurney was glad to see the director and even happier to see Welles, who certainly deserved to take a few bows for producing Carioca—yet didn't appear to be taking any. It impressed Gurney that he could be outraged at Welles' behavior at one moment and delighted with him at others, such as this.

The composer soon began to pace up and down, as though he were a schoolboy with a guilty secret; finally, he confessed that Carioca was in serious trouble with the government over a recent stock manipulation and might, at any moment, be put under arrest.

"Oh, Jesus Christ," said Hartog, sinking his head into his hands.

"What can I do, fellas," said Welles. "I tried."

At four o'clock in the afternoon, Welles flicked on the TV set in Undertag's office. Sure enough, after some brief coverage of student riots in Caracas, a handcuffed Hal Carioca appeared on the screen, grinning sheepishly as he was taken into custody by two federal agents.

"It looks like they got him," said Welles unnecessarily. "There goes our show."

"I don't know if I can take any more of this," said Hartog, with a profound and wounded groan.

At that point, Undertag skipped into the office and did a little two-step behind his desk.

"It's all right, fellas," he said, "we're in business. I just talked to my bank and I'll be goddamned if the sonofabitch's check didn't clear."

Even with the three hundred thousand in hand, Philip Undertag was infuriatingly laggard about moving ahead with plans for the show. Hartog and Gurney cornered him one day and told him quite frankly that it was time for him to get off his ass.

A key difficulty, he said, was getting just the right theatre for *Violencia.* The season ahead was a heavy one; each of the desirable houses appeared to be booked for an incoming show. Undertag, pinned to the wall that day by Gurney and Hartog, stared out of his window and arranged his mouth in a curious, thin-lipped, almost bitter style. He said that he and Toileau had arranged to purchase a massive amusement arcade in the Broadway area, with the idea of converting it into a legitimate theatre. Before making his move, Undertag had brought in sound experts from Berlin for an evalution. They said that even though the arcade had been used for children's games and the hawking of second-rate Broadway tourist merchandise, it was, amazingly, the most acoustically perfect building in the Western Hemisphere. Construction was moving forward. The theatre would be ready to accommodate *Violencia* when the show returned from its out-of-town engagements. Undertag had tried to keep his plan a secret, but several Broadway producers had gotten wind of it and tried to book the theatre-to-be (tentatively called the "Pokerino") for their own shows.

"I was tempted to lease it out, believe me," he said through thin lips, "but I told them, may God forgive me, I was going with *Violencia.*"

The producer advised Gurney and Hartog to stay away from the theatre for a while, since the children's games were still in operation; the two creators might be upset by the sight of youngsters at play in the future home of their show.

"But there's no point in losing the income," said Undertag. "We can keep the game concessions going until they're ready to put in the seats."

When Norman Welles heard about "The Pokerino," he ignored Undertag's advisory. With Tito Passionato in tow, he raced over to the arcade as fast as he was able to. Gurney, out of curiosity, tagged along and listened as the composer sang snatches of his songs from different parts of the huge, noisy arcade, with Passionato humming in the background.

Welles said he was something of a sound expert himself.

"And I'm not having one note of my songs lost in the wings, either. Not after I've broken my balls to write them."

After he had sung from several dozen locations in the enormous arcade, he shook his head in that appealingly boyish manner of his and declared that as far as he was concerned there wasn't a single dead spot in the entire Pokerino.

Since the theatre would not be ready for several months, auditions for *Violencia* got under way in Undertag's office. This was an exciting time for Gurney, who got to see the dicks and hookers and hoods he had created jump off the page in the form of live actors. There was no shortage of applicants, either. It seemed that every performer in the country wanted to work for Clement Hartog. A change came over the director at this point, too, which Gurney felt was a welcome one. Whereas Hartog's manner had been gentle and reticent in the work on the libretto, it now became deep-throated, majestic, and stentorian. He conducted the auditions with power and command, though he was capable of a soft word here and there when an auditioning actor appeared to be frightened and uncertain.

The key Chief of Homicide role, of course, was no problem, since it was by prearrangement to be played by the director's mother. Other principal parts included the young, socially enlightened detective hero, his one-armed girlfriend (a loving homage, he realized after he'd created the character, to his new friend, Angela), and the tricky role of the black dick with a compulsion to kill pantspressers. The pursuit of this fellow, his capture, and his subsequent fate in so many ways lay at the heart of *Violencia.*

Hartog felt that these would be difficult roles to cast and that the focus, at first, should be on the casting of relatively minor characters, which might go quickly.

"With a few of those under our belts, we'll feel better."

Hartog insisted that a stage manager be retained, to set up and run the auditions. Although Undertag fought him on this, the producer finally relented and hired an elderly pro named "Mr. Mortimer" who had managed shows dating all the way back to Ziegfeld.

"This is a big victory for us, Paul," said Hartog. "I want to see the sonofabitch spend. The deeper in he gets, the harder it will be for him to duck out on us."

Each auditioning actor was asked to do a dramatic scene for Hartog, a little dance for the Balinese choreographer, Han Nihsu, and finally, a song for Norman Welles, preferably one that the composer had written. At first the collaborators saw only young boys, filing in by the dozens from all parts of the globe. This was in deference to Mr. Mortimer, who would bring each one forth and say: "I think this young man would be wonderful for the panty-sniffing microAnalysis dick or perhaps for the polygraph expert. And I want you to know that I for one don't care whether he gets the part or not. I just think he'd be excellent, that's all."

Gurney was a little annoyed by this procedure, since it was obvious to him that none of Mr. Mortimer's young friends made any sense in the roles for which they were auditioning. But Hartog said it was just a ritual that had to be endured if you wanted the experienced Mr. Mortimer on the team.

"He knows all these boys from various beaches around the world, and he feels an obligation to them. Once he sees he can't slip them past us he'll start bringing in some real actors."

After Mr. Mortimer's acquaintances had been gotten out of the way, the professionals did have their turn. This was a thrilling experience for Gurney, seeing an actor, for example, who could be even more violent and homicidal than the many-gunned dick whose role he was trying to land.

Along with the acting, singing, and dancing requirements, Hartog, for some reason lodged deeply in his long experience, wanted each performer to be a crack shot and an expert in hand-to-hand combat. After the vocal auditions, the actors were given marksmanship tests in the basement of the Undertag Building and asked to throw Mr. Mortimer to the ground.

Following weeks of painstaking, often wearying auditions, most of the minor roles were cast; to everyone's considerable surprise and relief, a young black actor appeared who gave every indication that he would be superb in the complex role of the dick who is unmasked as a killer of pants-pressers. A mild-mannered, good-looking youth offstage, the actor, Hobie Hancock, gave an audition that was both beautiful and terrifying to watch. Mr. Mortimer had asked actors competing for the role merely to indicate that they were chained to a radiator. Hancock, however, insisted on actually finding one in Undertag's office, tearing it loose, and chaining himself so tightly to it that blood ran from his shoulders. For his song, he did "White Christmas," punching out each of the "whites" with bitter irony. His dancing was effortless, his marksmanship impeccable, and although he was slim of build, he was able to throw the shambling Mr. Mortimer farther than any of the previous applicants had.

"I won't mince any words with you," said Hartog, jumping up from his seat in excitement. "The part is yours if you want it."

"Hold on just a moment," said the quiet-spoken young man. "Let me audition *you.*"

"Go right ahead," said Hartog, somewhat brusquely.

"What is my motivation for wasting all those dry-cleaning personnel?"

"I'm not sure," Gurney put in defensively. "We're working on it."

"And Paul will get it, too," Norman Welles put in. "He's brilliant."

"Ever get your favorite suit ruined by a pants-presser?" Hartog volunteered. "With a major party coming up?"

"Then this is a comedy, right?" said Hancock thoughtfully.

"With serious undertones," Gurney shot back.

"My reference was to the *over*tones," Hancock replied. The actor reflected for a moment.

"I'll do your show," he said finally. "It's time I had something facetious in my life."

Hartog and Gurney saw hundreds of actors for the role of the young detective hero, but no one who was absolutely on target. Hartog suggested that perhaps it would be a good idea for the two of them to go out to the West Coast, where many of the best young performers were working in television. Gurney had never seen that part of the country. The prospect of flying to Los Angeles and perhaps mingling with people in the film colony was an exciting one.

"I'll pay your way out there, fellas," said Undertag, who had initially resisted the idea, "but only if you pay your way back."

In the days remaining before the scheduled trip, Gurney spent some of his time sitting in on Han Nihsu's chorus auditions. The celebrated Balinese choreographer, famed in theatre circles for her delicate pagoda-like ballet formations, put a great emphasis on buttocks, particularly when it came to the young female dancers. After her assistants, a quartet of young Balinese boys, had put each dancer through various movements, Han Nihsu would say impatiently: "All right, all right, turn her around and let me get a look at her ass."

"I can't stand a droopy tush on the stage," she later explained to Gurney. "There's no excuse for it. I'd rather not work than put up with a jelly-butt—or maybe do films, where you can fake it."

Each time she passed Gurney—as if to emphasize this concern of hers—she would back into the ex-dick and let him sample her aging but still firmed-up Asian behind, the kind she thought everyone should have.

Welles, a fitness nut, suddenly became concerned about his own ass, which he felt was losing its tone.

"Do you have any excercises for it?" he asked.

"Yes," said Han Nihsu. " We can do them together, but we'll have to cut our lunch periods short."

"I'd like to get started immediately," said Welles, reaching round to check himself for slackness.

Clement Hartog was a big booster of Han Nihsu's and had fought to get her hired for *Violencia.*

"No question, there will be a definite Asian flavor to the dances, but I think it's a good fit for our show. And the key thing is, Han is loyal and will go to the moon and back for us."

Gurney noted that Hartog preferred to work with people who would be willing to go to the moon—or through a brick wall—for him. The ex-homicider wondered if he himself would go that far, if asked to do so.

When the female dancers were finally chosen, Gurney was pleased to see that of the six taken, there were at least two cute ones and one marginal. Norman Welles was in on the final selection. He asked Gurney if he'd picked one for the out-of-town tryouts.

"They go crazy on the road from all the boredom, and love nothing more than to be entertained and screwed in your suite, since their own rooms are so pitifully small. Let me know which one you want, Paul, I'll tell you mine, and that way we'll make sure there's no conflict."

Gurney felt that Welles' plan was a bit callous, but he thanked him all the same. With a bitter chuckle, Hartog said that unfortunately he would be out of action, since Essie was in the show.

"She'll be watching me like a hawk."

The director took a special interest in the male dancers and was present at each audition to make sure that no conspicuously effeminate types were chosen.

"Normally, I woldn't be concerned. But we can ill afford that stuff in this particular show."

It was his idea that each performer in *Violencia* should look as though he or she belonged in or around a homicide bureau. Gurney could not really appraise the dance movements, but he was satisfied that each of the men selected was rugged and masculine-looking and might easily have passed for either a dick or a hood. Later, after they had all been signed up, he passed the office that had been used as a temporary dressing room and was surprised to see the six male dancers lounging around in masses of costume jewelry, several of them trying on Victorian dresses from an old Undertag production that had bitten the dust after two performances. In among the dancers was Hobie Hancock, who was twirling about in a dirndl. Gurney was somewhat rattled by all of this and reported what he had seen to Clement Hartog.

"Oh well," said the director with a sigh. "As long as they don't carry on during the performance."

At Hartog's insistence, a press agent was hired for *Violencia,* although Undertag fought the director on this, insisting there was no point in spending the money when the show might go directly down the tubes. As a compromise, Undertag hired a woman named Nettie

Hersel who was new to the business and in no position to command substantial fees. Just before Gurney left for the West Coast, the PR woman called and suggested they meet for lunch, with the idea of developing a few leads to promote the show.

"You could do with a little exposure," she told him over the phone. "You're a complete unknown."

They met at a theatrical restaurant where lesser lights in the business were summarily shipped off to the second floor. The head-waiter, predictably, showed Gurney the stairs to the upper tier.

"See what I told you?" said Nettie Hersel, trailing along behind him. "We have to sit in Siberia."

Gurney was more than a little irritated by her manner. His feelings certainly didn't change when she sat down and said that quite frankly she didn't think the show had a single redeeming feature— the characters were hateful, the music dreary, and the basic theme distasteful and outmoded.

"Don't worry, though. If I can come up with some angles, I'll work my butt off anyway. Personal feelings never get in the way of my job. I could have promoted Goebbels and never batted an eyelash. But I thought it was important to lay my feelings out on the line, so you won't think I'm a hypocrite. The show stinks to the high heavens."

Gurney hit the ceiling at this and went right after her.

"What about you?" he said. "What makes you so great? I hear you've never even done a goddamned show before. Who cares about your opinion?"

Nettie Hersel took a deep drag on her cigarette and, as if she were out on a first date, said, "Oh, I was a suburban housewife, and I was bored, bored, bored, what can I tell you. I tried cheating on my husband a few times, but that was only a temporary giggle. So now I'm doing this. Let's stop fooling around. Any scandal in your life, any dirt that we can slyly exploit?"

Although Gurney thought she was the worst woman he had

ever met, he was strangely unable to leave the table. And it wasn't because she was fascinating, either.

"There's no scandal," he said.

"Anything on Hartog?"

"You'll have to ask him."

"Now look," she said, with a kind of toughness that would have been more appropriate at Gurney's old bureau, "if you're not going to cooperate . . ."

"Who said I won't? But isn't there a decent way to publicize this show? How about the fact that I'm an ex-dick doing a libretto for a Broadway musical?"

"*Garbahge,*" said Nettie Hersel, giving the word a nauseating French twist. "And boy, do I ever pick 'em," she added over her shoulder, as though looking for support.

She puffed her cigarette down to the end and seemingly regained her composure.

"All right . . . there may be one stunt we can pull. It's worked for a few of my other clients, who, incidentally, are given tables downstairs when they come in here, and not shown directly to the toilet."

"It just might interest you to know," said Gurney, wishing he could be more acerbic, "that there are some people who come to this restaurant for the food."

"Good for them."

She then said that in her experience a surefire way of getting wide publicity was for the client in question to appear on one of the widely viewed late-night television talk shows with his or her mother, the two exchanging amusing anecdotes about one another and more or less appearing as a team.

"If by some miracle I can get you or your mom on one of them, I think Vio-luhnz-ic or whatever the hell you call it might have a prayer of getting some attention."

"My mother's dead."

"Oh, fuck," said Nettie Hersel.

"Fuck you," said Gurney.

"I'm glad I'm having lunch with such a gentleman."

Her voice was shaky as she said this, and she pulled a tissue out of her purse to dab at her eyes.

"If you're going to be hard-nosed," said Gurney, "you'd better develop a tougher hide."

But even as he spoke, he found himself feeling sorry for the woman. It seemed to be built into his character: feeling sympathy for people who'd insulted him and probably didn't deserve it. No doubt this was the driving spirit behind certain terrific religions, which he planned to investigate, as soon as he had a little spare time.

The night before Gurney left for California, as if to sweeten the Nettie Hersel experience, Philip Undertag called him at home and told him to drop everything and come right over to see the Pokerino.

"It's just about completely built now. The *Violencia* sign is up on the marquee, which has got to be a thrill for you.

"But you'd better take a look at it now," he added, "since this may be as far as the show will ever get."

Oddly enough, on this occasion, the last remark did not bother Gurney. He had gotten accustomed to Undertag's style, a combination of waspishness and perversity that was only half-serious. Then, too, the constant negative approach, intended or not, was probably a natural outgrowth of all those endless gray years of producing turkey after turkey. Additionally, when Undertag spoke, it was somewhat in the style of the typical boss: Never compliment the help or they might ask for more money. It was reminiscent of Gurney's old superior at the Bureau, Detective Turner, whose only reaction to the successful wrapping up of a brutal and maddeningly complex homicide was an infuriating little shrug, as if to imply that any idiot could have solved the case.

Much more important to Gurney at the moment was the fact that Undertag had been thoughtful enough to call him. Who could tell—perhaps the wealthy producer had a secret fondness for *Violencia,* but kept his enthusiasm hidden for fear of jinxing the show and killing off what might turn out to be his first hit since entering the business.

Gurney raced over in a cab. When he saw the Pokerino, all lit up, with the *Violencia* sign proudly displayed on its marquee, he asked the driver to slow down, and then to drive back and forth several times.

"It's a little show I'm doing," he said to the driver.

"Really? You don't look like an actor."

"No, no, I'm the author."

"Is that right?" said the driver. "Good luck to you. I once had Sammy Davis in the car."

Inside the Pokerino, Clement Hartog and Undertag stood in the midst of a group of carpenters who were working overtime to get the interior ready.

"How's she look?" asked the producer, who was beaming.

"How's she look?" Gurney repeated. "She looks great."

Indeed, he loved every seat in the theatre; he loved the carpeting, the overhead chandeliers, and he loved the half-completed stage. As far as he was concerned, he could have moved right in and lived there for the rest of his life. Up on the stage, Philip Undertag, with his hands in his pockets, stood facing an invisible audience, as if he were Gielgud about to deliver a soliloquy. He did his trademark curtsy and then, unaware that he was being watched, performed an economical little dance step, ending with a buck-and-wing and a bow. Gurney saw clearly then why the homely little man kept investing hundreds of thousands in show after show, even though he'd never gotten a penny in return.

"It's a wonderful feeling," said Gurney, who was flushed with enthusiasm as he strode up to the producer. "This has been quite a thrill for me. And I swear to Christ I mean that, even if we don't get a step further with the show."

"Bite your tongue, fella," said the producer. "And watch your ass in California."

ACT TWO

Scene 7

In the sky, being yanked from one side of the country to the other, Gurney had an excited but also dizzying, uncertain feeling, as if a support system had been snatched away. Months previous, he had been a clerk in a homicide bureau with a gray future. Now he was sitting beside the famed director Clement Hartog, flying west on a talent hunt for a homicidal musical comedy which was scheduled to open on Broadway in the fall. Yet for all the capricious nature of recent events, Gurney noticed that for the first time in his life he was not getting nauseous during a plane flight; it was as if his stomach was lined with new confidence.

Hartog sat beside him and seemed to be aging by the minute. Unable to relax, he had a wolflike expression on his face.

"I just hope we get a boy," said Hartog. "That's the only way I'll feel better. We've got to find someone who is substantial enough to stand up to Essie. She can blow most people off the stage. And when she's on her stilts, it's every man for himself."

A massive ship-sized limousine was at the airport to greet them, supplied by Hunt Feur, who had heard that Hartog and Gurney were rolling into town. The starlet who had been assigned to Hartog on the East Coast was on hand to greet the director once again. A sullen, somewhat older starlet was present as well, presumably as an escort for Gurney.

"You want to know the shitty part?" said the driver, wheeling around to talk to the two collaborators as he steered them along La Cienega to their hotel. "I've been trying to break into the business for twenty-eight years, in any capacity—actor, electrician, I'm even willing to be an agent. And yet you two guys breeze in for the first time and they hand you the town on a platter."

The comments seemed to be directed particularly to Hartog, who was exchanging noisy embraces with his starlet and sneaking a hand beneath her dress. Gurney, who was less interested in the woman who sat beside him, replied on the director's behalf.

"Mr. Hartog is one of the greatest figures in the entertainment world," he said importantly. "He isn't some kid off the street, if that's what you're getting at."

"What about you?"

Gurney was caught off guard by the question.

"I'm doing fine," he said vaguely, in a lame attempt to encase himself in mystery. "Don't worry about me."

At the hotel, Gurney and Hartog were shown to separate quarters. Gurney was astonished when he saw the suite of rooms that had been prepared for him—three bedrooms, a massive terraced parlor, a full kitchen, and more bathrooms with stall showers than he could ever hope to use.

"Good God," he said to the bellman, "you could stage a convention in here."

"We're not permitted to talk politics," the man replied.

An enormous bouquet of rare tropical flowers had been set up for Gurney in the sitting room, along with silvered bowls of fruit, dripping with freshness and moisture. There was a card in one of them.

"For Paul Gurney, who we are betting on to hit it big with *Violencia* and who we hope will follow with a passel of pictures for our studio."

Henny Gelb, Head of Story Development,
Apollinaire Productions

Gurney thought it was extraordinary that the studio would make such a long-range bet on a total newcomer—and he felt awkward about using the enormous suite. For example, he could only get himself to settle into one bedroom and bathroom. Upon reflection, however, he saw that even though the amount of money involved in making him comfortable seemed outlandish, it was a mere pittance in terms of the many millions spent by Apollinaire on developing projects—many of them doomed from the start. The insight helped him to relax a bit and to enjoy several more of the bathrooms.

Hartog paid him a visit before dinner.

"Holy Christ," he said after a look around, "just look at what they've done for you. They've got me in a crappy little corner suite with only two bedrooms and no terrace.

"Say now," he said, with more than a trace of sarcasm, "they must really think you're something. I've done eight pictures for this studio and they treat me like a slob."

"This is preposterous," said Gurney. "I insist that you move in here and I'll take the crappy little suite they gave you."

"Uh-uh," said Hartog, refusing to let him off the hook. "You stay right where you are. I didn't realize I was with such an important fellow.

"And fruit, too," he said, picking up a pear with two fingers, then dropping it back in the bowl. "I didn't even get a can of sardines."

*   *   *

Hunt Feur had arranged for the two collaborators to have dinner with him at the legendary Chasen's restaurant, along with Hartog's pretty young starlet and Gurney's venerable one. No sooner had they taken seats at their booth than Feur presented Hartog with a small bejeweled pair of binoculars and a silk bathrobe. Then he went right after Gurney.

"I see your boy here is the darling of the studio," he said to Hartog.

"Yes," Hartog agreed. "From the way they're treating him, you'd think he was Orson Welles."

The two then exchanged knowing Central European chuckles.

"This royal treatment wasn't my idea," said Gurney, who was annoyed at the director for siding with Feur. " I'd just as soon come and go anonymously until I do something to deserve it."

"And how exactly do you plan to stand our little industry on its ear?" asked Feur, becoming oilier by the minute.

Before Gurney could choke out a response, Henny Gelb, the fellow who had arranged the elegant suite for him, arrived and took a seat in the booth. He was a young fellow who had begun his career as a New Jersey shingles salesman and who through sheer bluff, ingenuity, personal charm, and ruthlessness had bulled his way into a key position at Apollinaire. At the moment, the company was the hot film company on the Coast.

Once Gelb appeared, Hunt Feur became subdued. The elder Viennese was doing several pictures for Apollinaire; in a sense, he was beholden to, if not actually employed by, the young fellow.

Gurney looked around the restaurant and recognized filmdom greats who had thrilled him as a young boy. Gurney had never missed Saturday afternoons at the movies, and he and his ex-wife had once agreed that the reason for their breakup was that they had learned all of their behavior at the movies: Gurney met life in the style of Bogart, Gary Cooper, Dick Powell, and George Brent; Gilda Gurney could not face difficult situations unless she had seen Linda Darnell or Cyd Charisse tackle the same ones on the screen.

It was unbelievable to Gurney, but unless he was mistaken, several of the film personalities at the restaurant kept craning their necks forward and keeping an ear cocked for tidbits they might overhear at his table. Actually, they weren't talking shop at all. Gelb wanted to know if the ex-dick was satisfied with the arrangements.

"Look around," he said, with the two starlet escorts listening attentively, "and let me know if there's any young puss here that interests you."

Gurney had actually been aware of several strikingly attractive young women who were seated in an adjoining booth—and whom he took to be actresses. Still, he insisted that Gelb had gone to enough trouble already and needn't bother to do any more.

"Nonsense," said Gelb, glancing over at the two women and making a notation on a pad. "Most of them are under contract to us. I'll have them shipped in and out of your room like running water."

Gurney could not help but admire young Henny Gelb's way of catering nakedly and unashamedly to basic instincts. And he saw clearly why the recently unknown salesman had been able to go from shingles to the top of the film colony.

Gelb took the group to a popular discotheque and immediately upon arrival invited Gurney to scout around and see if there were any other girls he wanted to add to the list. Gurney did not actually feel any hunger for women at the moment, but thought he might as well take advantage of the opportunity. After all, he was on the West Coast and in the thick of the movie business; passing it by would be like traveling to a city famed for its art treasures and not visiting any of the museums.

Perhaps understandably, the woman who had been assigned to Gurney as an escort became irritable and complained about the temperature in the club.

"I feel a terrible draft. Can't someone check the windows and make sure they're shut tight?"

Gurney asked a waiter to see what he could do—and then turned to Clement Hartog's date, who interested him. He asked her to dance and she said she'd be delighted. But on the floor, when he tried to gather her in close, she drew back and held him at arm's length.

"Now look, Mr. Feur's instructions are that I am only to fuck Mr. Hartog. If Mr. Gelb had gotten to me first, I would have been able to fuck you, Mr. Gurney, but he didn't, and I don't want to lose my contract with Mr. Feur."

"I understand completely," said Gurney. "Don't give it a second thought."

He finished the dance with her, trying all the while to charm her out of the arrangement—but she refused to budge. He ended up telling himself that he did not want to make love to someone who was that cold, even though she had a great body. An hour later, when the others in the party made ready to leave, Gurney said he'd like to stick around and have a drink in solitude, then catch a cab back to the hotel.

"You writers," said Gelb, clucking his tongue and taking out a pad and pencil. "Let me take down that 'solitude' remark. I can tell I'm going to use that somewhere."

Gurney had a few brandies and decided he didn't enjoy being alone after all. He went back to the sumptuous suite, expecting a few of the actresses he had pointed out to be there, but none showed up. After an hour or so of waiting for them to appear, he concluded that Gelb really meant the following night; still, he was hungover and lonely, so he called Angela at what must have been four-thirty in the morning for her—and told her that he loved her. It was unfair of him to say this, since he didn't know if he meant it or if it was coming out of loneliness. And to pull that on a one-armed girl, too. Unless you were sincere, it was a cruel thing to do.

* * *

Gurney had only one friend on the West Coast, a young, intelligent ex-dick who had given up homicide and gone west to become a chiropractor. The fellow had been living in the Beverly Hills area with his mother and from all reports had prospered mightily. His name was Matt Tanker. Gurney wanted at least one person to see his lavish hotel quarters and verify its existence, so the next day he called the ex-dick.

Tanker came right over, and brought his mother along. Gurney had room service prepare a delicious lunch for them, courtesy of Apollinaire.

"Matt and I think it's wonderful that you've hit it big in films," said Mrs. Tanker, a heavily suntanned woman who was weighted down with costume jewelry. "We always knew you had it in you when we saw you brooding around the Bureau, as if you had other things on your mind.

"Of course," she said, beaming at her son, "Matt takes real good care of his mom . . . and I'm sure you do the same for yours."

Gurney reminded Mrs. Tanker that his mother was dead.

"I'm sorry, I must have forgotten," she said, patting his hand. "But if you like, I can be a mother to both of you boys."

She then told Gurney about the many admirers she had on the Coast and how they preferred her to younger women, even starlets.

"They take out the young ones and then they return to me and say: 'Maureen has a beautiful behind, but just try talking to a *tochis*.'"

Tanker had been a good son to his mother, perhaps passing up married life so he could be her constant companion; his situation, curiously, ran parallel to that of Clement Hartog and *his* mom, Essie.

It seemed, upon further thought, that everyone Gurney knew was seriously involved with his mother. Perhaps it was in the air.

Mrs. Tanker thanked Gurney for lunch and then went off to meet one of her young beaux, leaving the two ex-dicks to reminisce about old times.

Gurney recalled that Matt Tanker had been a highly decorated sex patroller and had always been teased for wearing extra-flashy ties. He looked handsome and fit and without exaggeration a good ten years younger than he had when he'd been working at the Bureau.

"California certainly has been good to you, Matt," said Gurney.

Tanker thanked Gurney and said he now operated a small clinic that ran alongside a dangerous canyon in the Hollywood Hills. Through a good-buddy arrangement with local police, accident victims, some of whom had gone plunging into the canyon, were referred to the Tanker Clinic for treatment of their back injuries.

Gurney had not been all that close to Tanker at the bullpen, but he had to admit it was great running into the ex-homicider some three thousand miles from the old Bureau. That was one thing about law enforcers—they had a strong sense of fraternity and tended to both strike up new friendships and to renew old ones in no time at all. Though Gurney had only been a clerk in the Bureau, he was sure that he would always feel brotherly toward dicks, no matter how long he had been out of Homicide. And he could spot a dick in two seconds flat, by the way a man entered a restaurant, the manner in which he caught another man's eyes—or avoided them.

While chatting with his handsome friend, Gurney recalled that Tanker had once been interested in theatre, too. Unless he was mistaken, the former sex patroller had once played a small part in an all-dick production of *Kiss Me, Kate* as part of a fund-raiser for the widows of slain crime fighters.

"They gave me a shitty little part," said Tanker.

"You played Gremio," Gurney recalled. "You were terrific."

"Maybe," said Tanker with bitterness. "But my Petruchio would have brought down the house."

The *Violencia* auditions were scheduled for later that afternoon in downtown Los Angeles. Gurney suggested that his friend might enjoy them and want to put his head in. Tanker immediately brightened up. He said he wouldn't miss them for the world.

There was talent on the West Coast, all right. Within an hour after the auditions had begun, Gurney and Hartog saw that their trip had not been a useless one. They signed two youngsters on the spot as singers; in addition, they felt they'd come up with some "possibles" for the all-important hero detective who would play opposite Essie Hartog.

Matt Tanker, the homicide dick turned chiropractor, watched the proceedings with fascination, unconsciously tapping his feet when an energetic hopeful got something going.

"Who is that fellow?" Hartog had asked with suspicion. "And what is he doing here?"

Hartog did not want strangers around when he was working; Gurney guessed he was also a little jealous of anyone the librettist had as a friend. Gurney felt the same way about the director's closeness to Hunt Feur. But Gurney vouched for the former sex patroller, assuring Hartog that he was a highly decent individual.

"All right then," said the director. "Just make sure there isn't a peep out of him."

At the end of the day, the collaborators felt a small sense of accomplishment, although they had to admit the discouraging truth that they had not really found anyone who was absolutely right to play Essie Hartog's detective son.

Matt Tanker overheard them discussing their problem.

"Would you fellows mind if I tried a few numbers?"

"Sure," said Hartog, looking weary and skeptical.

No doubt this was out of courtesy to Gurney.

Tanker squatted down for a whispered exchange with the piano accompanist. Then the ex-homicider took the stage with a song-and-dance number from *42nd Street*. He certainly was light on his feet, Gurney felt, and there was no denying his charm, though he had a tendency to overuse it and perhaps punch a little too hard. Hartog continued to look bored and uninterested, but began to sit up and pay attention when Tanker did a lazy ballad from *Brigadoon,* displaying a surprisingly rich and—even more important—relaxed, authentic musical comedy voice. And then Tanker set both collaborators back on their heels with his final number, a rock-'em-sock-'em rhythm tune from a musical review that had died in Philadelphia years back, despite having the one great number in it.

Gurney and Hartog found themselves on their feet, applauding with genuine enthusiasm. *And it's not just because he's my old friend,* Gurney told himself.

"How long have you been studying?" Hartog asked the former sex patroller after he had left the stage, huffing and puffing and drenched with perspiration.

"Not too long, sir," said Tanker, falling into a seat. "About a year here in L.A. and on and off with my mom, who's a vocal coach."

Sensing that something extraordinary was about to happen, Gurney was glad that Tanker was being so polite and deferential to Hartog. He recalled that his friend had always been gentle and soft-spoken during pervert investigations, too, saying "sir" to the worst degenerates in town. The training had prepared him well for a career in show business.

"Paul says you have a booming practice out here on the Coast," said Hartog. "Would you give it all up to come east?"

"To do a Broadway show, sir? In a New York minute."

"You're awfully good," said Hartog with an appreciative little shake of his head. "I have to admit you caught me off guard, it being the end of a long day and you suddenly auditioning and all that. But good is good . . . and you're awfully good."

"Thank you, sir," said Tanker.

"Let Paul and I talk it over," said Hartog. "We'll be in touch. Who's your agent, by the way?"

"I guess it's my mom," said the ex-dick with a sheepish grin that warmed up the room, and that Gurney figured would probably come across effectively on the stage as well.

"Look, Clement," said Gurney after his friend had left, practically sailing out of the theatre, "I don't want my friendship with Tanker to have anything whatever to do with his being considered for the part."

"Oh, I know that, Paul," said Hartog.

He put his hand on Gurney's knee and looked him in the eye with great understanding. Gurney appreciated the gesture.

"I *do* think he's good," said Hartog. "He's a little old, but in that area, you're allowed to fudge somewhat on the stage. Then, too, I realize he punches too hard and would have to be toned down, but I think I can get a performance out of him. And you have something special going for you when you bring in a complete unknown, especially if he sizzles."

"I feel all the same things about him," said Gurney, "but I want to be absolutely sure my judgment isn't being clouded. After all, we were in homicide together. No matter how hard you try to minimize that, it's got to be a factor."

"Tell you what," said Hartog, after a moment or two of silent consideration.

"What?"

"Let's fly him east."

Scene 8

When the two collaborators got back home, their first or der of business was to wrap up the casting so they could get on with rehearsals before Undertag got cold feet and decided to back away from the show.

"I think he's afraid he's got a hit on his hands," said Hartog. "This is a new experience for him and he'll probably do everything in his power to kill it off. When I think of how we brought the sonofabitch pure gold, and he doesn't even see it."

There were two key parts that remained to be filled, those of the detective hero son Matt Tanker, soon to fly east, was at the head of the pack for that one and his one-armed ingenue girlfriend at the Bureau. Mr. Mortimer lined up all of the available young one-armed actresses in the city; Gurney was surprised that there were so many of them. The part finally went to a pretty and feisty little bundle of talent named Betty Pound. She was acknowledged to be over-brimming with talent, but understandably, she had found it rough going in the theatre because of the shortage of parts for girls with one wing.

Gurney was not fooling himself; he knew that the charac-ter was based on a real-life individual, his dear friend Angela. And his heart fell when he saw the audition of Betty Pound, who was slightly prettier than Angela and was certainly a better singer and dancer. What if he became romantically involved with Betty Pound? But he was almost relieved to discover that the actress's good qualities were all playacting ones. Offstage, her personality was a brittle and unappealing one. She was obsessed with only one goal in life: success in the theatre, and after that, Hollywood.

When Matt Tanker flew east, the two collaborators sat him down for a final interview and gave him a thorough going-over.

"This is a long, tough haul," said Hartog. "You've been a sex detective and a chiropractor. What makes you so sure you can cut it as the lead in a Broadway musical?"

To his credit, Tanker refused to beg and plead for the part. With his mother at his side, he sat opposite the two of them, clear-eyed, pleasant, steady.

"I don't know that I can, sir, but I'd sure like to try. If it doesn't work out, I can either go back to my practice or perhaps find an island in the Pacific and just sit around and count the waves."

Since the time they had seen him on the West Coast, Tanker had let his hair grow out. He was wearing torn blue jeans, moccasins, and a dirty old poncho that was falling apart.

"I don't know," said Hartog, taking Gurney aside. "I still like him, but I prefer an actor who'll fight and claw and insist that he's the only one in the world who can do the part and tell us that if we don't agree we can go fuck ourselves."

"I know what you mean," said Gurney. "He doesn't seem to have as much desire as I would have thought."

"Do you think that no other actor could do this except you?" the director asked, returning to Matt Tanker's side.

"No, sir," said Tanker, calm, flap-proof, polite. "I think there are many others who probably can, too. And if you decide against me, I won't be in the least upset. I'd be happy to take some lowly job as a chorus boy. And I'd consider myself lucky to have come this far."

The director motioned Gurney to step aside with him once again.

"He certainly makes it hard on you, doesn't he? But oh well, let's hire him. If he doesn't pan out, we can always can his ass on the road."

Now that the casting had been rounded off, Hartog insisted that Undertag hire several other key professionals for the *Violencia* team. Hartog got the producer to go along with Bess Filimino on sets; high-priced and difficult to get along with, she believed in keeping her sets vivid but minimal. It was her theory that a single .45-caliber cartridge, if properly placed on the stage and set up emotionally by the script, could take the place of an entire homicide bureau, and might even turn out to be twice as effective.

In order to get the set designer of his choice, Hartog had to go along with the producer and hire Rolf Rienzo, who came cheap on costumes. Once famed for his papal vestments in religious spectacle plays, Rienzo had suffered a mental collapse and been packed off to Swiss clinics to recuperate.

"It's all right," the director told Gurney as if there were a need to calm him down. "Rolf hasn't worked for years and he's still a little shaky. But he's not bad, and I think he's got another show in him. If we keep a careful eye on him, I believe he'll perform for us."

For musical conductor, Norman Welles would hear of no one but Ty Sabatini, a man who made sense in the economy department, too, since he could imitate every instrument in the pit, from saxophones to entire woodwind sections. When Gurney met him, the conductor struck him as being both pompous and suspicious, salting his remarks with a blend of foreign expressions such as "andante," "fortissimo," "che bella" "tout de suite," and "m'love." But after a while, Gurney saw that this style was only a defensive mannerism; once he let his hair down, Sabatini was really a sweet and decent man, another individual who—in Hartog's words—would go to the moon for you.

The conductor also struck Gurney as being a bit fearful of writers, perhaps because his own world was filled entirely by musical sounds. To express himself, Sabatini, typically, might say something like, "If we *zunnng* it and give it some *pnunng* and *dadootdadootzazay,* we'll be home free."

One of Sabatini's functions, during rehearsals, was to work with Essie Hartog on the development of her voice, tailoring it particularly to the Pokerino, with its huge balconies and enormous ceilings. Essie reacted poorly to Sabatini at first.

"Why, you cheap, money-grubbing peasant cunt" was her initial address to him.

But Essie, too, quickly became aware of his great abilities and his warmth. In a turnabout, she declared, "There's no one in the world like him."

Once the full team had been assembled, Clement Hartog gathered together the cast and production staff for a first reading of the *Violencia* script. For the occasion, he wore a full-dress tuxedo with tails. Gurney, in jeans and a corduroy jacket, wondered if he should have dressed more formally as well. There was so much he had to learn about the ways of the theatre.

The director said he had worked on many shows before, but that he was never more proud in his life of a cast than he was of this one.

"For that matter, I've never come across a libretto that was better than that of *Violencia.*"

There was so much watery-eyed conviction in his delivery that Gurney, and probably everyone else who was there, believed his every word.

Gurney then introduced Philip Undertag, who skipped forward for a few words.

"As many of you know," said the producer, "I haven't had any hits, and God knows, the odds are against this being one. But I want you to know that if you keep your noses clean, this office is behind you. And if the show does work out, I'm giving everyone free piano lessons."

As the production staff and cast struggled to digest the strange offer, Hartog introduced each of them by name. To his astonishment, only Gurney and the talented Hobie Hancock drew substantial applause. Gurney didn't understand this, and certainly felt he'd done nothing to earn the tribute. But he had to admit it was a most enjoyable moment.

Gurney then saw Matt Tanker lean across to Norman Welles, not realizing that he was speaking to the composer.

"Don't you wish the music wasn't shit?" he said.

Welles, in total shock, managed a thin smile, and Gurney probably felt as bad about the gaffe as the composer. Even though he hadn't pushed for the hiring of Tanker, he accepted some responsibility for him. He was ashamed of the sex patroller's crudeness, and, for the moment, of their shared past. Was it possible that Tanker really knew that Welles was the composer—and that the outrageous frankness was part of some weird newly acquired West Coast style?

The cast then read through the script, the experienced ones going through it perfunctorily, just to get the feel of it. Essie delivered her lines in German. Gurney's heart sank when he heard the harsh Prussian sounds coming from the leading lady; right then and there he gave up on the show, deciding it did not have a chance on Broadway. Hartog, ever-considerate, and with an unerring directorial sense of exactly what was in the air, read the discomfort on his face.

He approached the young librettist and put an arm around him.

"Don't worry, Paul," he said. "It's just Essie's way of holding back, of concealing herself. It's a form of shyness, really. She'll drop the German soon enough, the minute she gets a little confidence going.

"You don't think for a second I'd let her *open* in German, do you? Boy, that would be the day."

Rehearsals were a free and irresponsible time for Gurney; in many ways, he wished they could go on forever. The libretto was completed; he guessed that if *Violencia* got slaughtered in the out-of-town notices, he would be called upon to make plenty of changes. But for the moment, there was nothing much for him to do but hang around and take little tastes of other people's work. On a typical day, he might watch Hartog take Essie through a scene, then pop in on Han Nihsu as she erected one of her delicate, symmetrical pagodas out of real chorus kids. He loved the look of them, although frankly he didn't see how they were going to fit into a show about violence in a homicide bureau.

The only other person who seemed to be idle was Normal Welles. As Gurney might have guessed, he planned to make very few changes in the romantic light love lyrics. The composer now took the tack that he would put the matter in the hands of the out-of-town critics.

"If they cut me to ribbons, there will be plenty of time to do fixes before we hit New York. After all, there's only one opening that really counts, the big one, right here on Broadway."

Welles spent his days sitting in the rear of the theatre wearing a big boyish grin. On one occasion, when Gurney took a seat beside him, Welles reached out and gave him a big hug.

"Isn't this great?" he said. "You can't imagine how it's going to feel being on Broadway. I love you, Paul. The two of us are very much alike and could be brothers, you know that. I'll change any lyric you want, but can't we wait, for Christ's sake, until we read the out-of-town notices? I can be wrong—dammit, anyone can— but I just don't think I am in this case."

Then, in a whisper, he said: "Clement Hartog is brilliant and we're fortunate to have him, but I happen to know that there's talk in some quarters that he may be slipping. His Hollywood price has dropped a couple of hundred thou per picture."

Gurney removed Welles' arm from his shoulder after hearing the remark—in that manner letting the composer know he wanted no part of any criticism of his colleague and friend.

If Welles and Gurney were loose and carefree though this period, Hartog seemed grim and concerned. Matt Tanker was a bright spot, picking up direction quickly, dropping many of his cute and self-conscious mannerisms, and generally behaving like an old pro. But the work with Essie Hartog was complex and exhausting. Though no one dared breathe a word of it, the fact of her being the director's mom was always in the air. It made Clement Hartog both too tough on her and too lenient. At times, he would force her to do her lines over and over until she fell into an exhausted heap, all the while, berating, insulting, and humiliating her, not caring who was present.

"Let's go, let's go, slutface," he would cry out. "What do you think this is, a picnic? If you can't do your lines that way, take off the fucking stilts, you bloody whore."

At other times, when she muffed a line, he would jump up on the stage and cradle her head.

"Whoosa matter, pussypie?" he'd ask while stroking her hair.

And at these moments, if he so much as sensed some criticism of her, perhaps from a stagehand, he would lash out at the often innocent fellow.

"Watch your ass, buster! I will not tolerate any of that in my theatre. Lest you've forgotten, this is my mother."

Gurney felt there was a purpose and design in Hartog's handling of Essie. But he also suspected that the director keenly felt the pressure of directing a close loved one in a Broadway musical that cost a fortune to get on. Wouldn't anyone?

If Essie was a problem for Hartog, the gifted Hobie Hancock was no prize either. Trained in a discipline called the Black Method, Hancock insisted on knowing the motivation for his every action and how it related to Black America. Why am I holding this gun, he would want to know, and can I justify it in terms of my blackness? Why am I spitting on the floor; why am I bleeding? Do my actions violate my black conscience? When he heard these questions, Hartog, sitting in the audience, would turn halfway around in his seat.

"Like I really need this," he would mumble. "What the fuck am I supposed to tell him?"

Hartog would then mount the stage and do his best to give the brilliant performer a useful answer.

Not only did Hartog have his hands full with the actors, but he also expressed certain nagging doubts about the *Violencia* libretto. He felt there were occasional dead spots, lapses in continuity, and hinted around that he wouldn't mind putting in some nights with Gurney on repairs. But somehow Gurney managed to slip away from him. He had gotten the impression that Hartog was a worrier and that for all his great success was a bit too finicky. It was awful to admit it, but for all of the love and respect he had for Hartog, he recognized in himself a certain contempt for the director as well. Gurney had done his work; why not let the old man struggle by himself for a while? It was a selfish attitude, and also an ironic one. From the beginning, Gurney had been resentful of Hartog and Norman Welles for all of their successes, their lavish homes, their fame, and their millions of dollars. He himself was an unknown, close-to-penniless former homicide clerk. In a sense, wasn't he being exploited by this group of privileged sonsofbitches, who could easily afford to work indefinitely for no assured return?

Yet he also saw that perhaps he was the morally suspect one. After all, the theatre was their work; they slaved at it and depended upon the stage not only for their fortunes but for their pride and their reputations. They were in it for blood. If *Violencia* failed, Norman Welles might never work in the theatre again. And Clement Hartog would find his reputation sorely tarnished. No matter what happened to the show, Gurney, with no reputation to lose, would simply go about his business, refreshed, invigorated by the experience. It was unlikely that he would be involved in a stage piece again. In a sense, wasn't he just tailing along for the fun of it? Hitching a ride on their energies and talent and not really playing for keeps? Wasn't he merely using *Violencia* as a pleasant way to pass a delicate, newly divorced interlude in his life? Make a few new friends, have a few chuckles, maybe sleep with a couple of dancers? Perfect evidence was the way in which he ducked out on Hartog each time the director suggested they put in some more hours on the libretto. Hartog was much older than Gurney and did the work of ten men during the day. But to get *Violencia* just right, he was willing to press on, round-the-clock if necessary. The old man was too proud to come out and plead with Gurney for help; but his eyes begged the younger man to pitch in. And there was the fear of a cornered animal in them, too.

Gurney saw all of this and ignored it.

Instead of rolling up his sleeves and helping out, he continued to scoop up the gravy.

For all of his cynicism and artful ducking of additional work, Gurney loved to wait for Clement Hartog after rehearsals so he could get a review of the day's progress. It was as though he had bought a high-flying stock and needed only to check it each day to see how much money he had made. The two men would join Han Nihsu and her nimble Balinese assistants for drinks at a Lebanese restaurant close to the Pokerino. The talk was rough, vulgar, rowdy, Hartog and Han Nihsu telling stories of past shows they had done. Gurney, loving the yarns, was mostly silent, since he of course had none to tell. But he enjoyed the closeness and camaraderie of it.

On one occasion, he saw Nicol, the proprietor, point to the *Violencia* table and tell several curious diners: "They're show folk, from the musical next door."

The people responded with a look of awed understanding, and Gurney loved being included in the group.

Another time, he complained to Han Nihsu about lack of sleep.

"If you don't like the hours," she said sharply, "who asked you to become a gypsy?"

So now he was a gypsy. The very word was staggering. It seemed the final accolade. While working at the Bureau, once in a while he'd felt a thin trickle of desire to be a suspect, rather than a good guy. There was hardly any comparison, but his membership in the little band of theatre people seemed to fulfill his desire to be some kind of outlaw.

On occasion, the chorus kids, too, came into the restaurant after work, but they took seperate tables, the protocol being that they did not sit with "management." Gurney wanted to be in their outsiders' group, too, which was peripheral to a group that was outside to begin with—and consequently had a certain mystique to it.

"We're just chorus kids," they would say, implying that they were unimportant and not to be taken seriously. But there was a reverse snobbery in their attitude.

One of them was a slender blonde girl named Holly who was something of a contortionist. She never stopped maneuvering and manipulating her body, even after work, twisting it into odd and somewhat inviting postures, sometimes in the restaurant. Norman Welles' friend, Tippy, as production assistant, was now a full-fledged member of the team; as such, she was aware of every bit of backstage intrigue, particularly the various romantic entanglements in-volving members of the cast. Taking Gurney aside one day, she con-fided that Holly was insane about him.

"She almost faints every time you walk by, or even when you enter a room."

Gurney had no idea the dancer/contortionist had such feel-ings about him, but he was pleased to hear that she did. He thought of calling her after work, but decided to hold off, for fear of throwing off the rehearsals and starting an affair that might distract her from her work and make the other girls jealous. There would be plenty of time out of town to scoop up the delightful and flexible little dancer.

On occasion, Essie Hartog would join the cast at the res-taurant and, much to her son's displeasure, quickly get pissed to the gills. She became quite coarse and vulgar, reverting to her old Berlin cabaret style, insulting members of the company without discrimi-nation. Han Nihsu was a favorite target.

"So you think you're going to make a dancer out of me, do you?" said Essie Hartog. "That'll be the day, you slant-eyed cunt."

Although Clement Hartog was the master of his mom on the stage, he seemed unable to handle her when she was in this con-dition. He would merely slump over pathetically and get quietly pissed along with her.

At one point, she seemed to sober up for a moment, grip-ping Gurney's leg and giving it a squeeze of encouragement.

"Don't worry, darling. I know how hard you've worked on this show. And if it kills me, I'm going to see to it that your precious lines are delivered with all the pain and agony and truth with which you wrote them."

She topped this off by kissing him on the cheek and crying into his neck and generally making him feel awful, since he hadn't worked on *Violencia* with any of the agony she referred to. As a matter of fact, quite to the contrary, he had done a pretty good job of goofing off, at least since rehearsals began.

He loved the tightness and fraternity of the little band. Only in one sense did he feel injured by it. There was no way to work in an outsider, and this held true for Angela, even though he felt closer to her than ever. When she came to the restaurant, the theatre people cleared a small space for her, but they weren't really making room for her at all. She had little to say and when she did speak, her brave remarks such as "I bought a great dress today" were out of joint and more or less special in the wrong way, as though a spotlight had been pointed at her. Still, she was very good and understanding about the way she was treated, taking whatever crumbs of attention that were available and happy enough simply to be with Gurney.

Only late at night, when he slept with her, was Gurney entirely comfortable with Angela. She took exquisite care of him, so much so that he began to think of her as a member of some tribe whose women are famed for never allowing their men to suffer erotic deprival. At the slightest sign of it, they would jump forth to drain it away in a single hawklike draft. At times, he would awaken to find her inches from him, cross-legged, sharp-eyed, watching his body for the slightest quiver of need, guarding him like a gypsy fire, her sacred, devotional duty being to see to it that he never got the least bit overhorny.

Occasionally, during rehearsals, she would take a seat in the extreme rear of the Pokerino. Now and then, Gurney, who every so often helped Hartog with the scene interpretations, would wander back to Angela and stroke her arm. Each time he did this, he had the odd and preposterous notion that his ex-wife had marched in to catch him at it; he would wheel around to make sure it wasn't true.

But one evening, Gilda Gurney actually did show up.

"I was just passing by," she said, "and I thought I'd say hello."

He let her watch some of the rehearsal, not introducing her to any of the cast and, to his discredit, feeling smug. It was as if he were saying: "See what you missed? See what you could have had if you'd been a devoted wife and not kept flirting with other dicks? Tough luck, Gilda. And I may not even take you to the opening, either. What do you think of that?"

The appearance in the theatre of Gurney's ex-wife made him think of his poor mother and what a thrill she would have had knowing that her son was involved in a Broadway show. Babs Gurney had become a heavy drinker in her last years. Barely able to get a coherent sentence out of her, he had finally thrown up his hands and stayed away from her. One night, after weeks of not speaking to her, he had called, and sure enough, she was totally out of it, babbling a lot of what he felt was nonsense. He hung up in a fury. *What a waste,* he'd thought. She had an excellent mind; they could have been such good friends if she hadn't spent all that time knocking them back. That was the night she died.

A neighbor reported that she'd been sober for a week and had been waiting for Gurney to call, to tell him what a "good girl" she'd been. But on the night of his call, Babs Gurney had begun to gasp for air; what Gurney had taken to be nonsensical blather had actually been the short-of-breath start of a heart attack and a desperate cry for help. That was a difficult time for Gurney. If the episode had come about at an earlier period of his life, he might have ended up in an institution, blanketed with guilt. But he pulled himself through, arguing that if she was sober on this particular night, she was in a stupor on a thousand others. He wasn't going to whip himself for a lifetime because he had chosen Babs Gurney's one good night to hang up on her.

It was slippery going, but he talked himself into all of this. And it was probably a lucky thing that he did.

For all of Gurney's cynical detachment from the actual work, and despite Hartog's many concerns, the show seemed to be coming together and marching forward on its own. Essie Hartog, who'd had some early difficulty picking up the beat and rhythm of the Homicide Chief's style, finally got the hang of it; both on and off the stage, she *was* the Chief, and in many ways, more tough and pigheaded than the character Gurney had contrived. Once Hobie Hancock made peace with the essential blackness of his role, and its importance to Black America, he too settled into his role. Matt Tanker took on the firm demeanor of the Homicide Chief's detective son, drawing, quite candidly, from his days as a vice dick who knew that the best way to get around a dangerous sexual weirdo was to treat the individual with some dignity.

Each member of the cast, in turn, began to settle into his or her homicidal role.

For Gurney, rehearsals were like being around a homicide bureau again, but one that was much more murderous and violent than any he had ever known. Each day, in the theatre, he heard the whine of bullets, the hiss of switchblades, the thwack of hard rubber coming down on heads. There was a constant scream of night sirens, coming from ambulances filled with bleeding hoods and wounded dicks.

One day, he could have sworn he heard police dogs barking savagely in the wings. He tracked down the sound and found its source in a small dressing room in the Pokerino basement. Though he opened the door cautiously, he almost had his throat torn out by three chained-up rottweilers.

"Why didn't someone tell me about this?" he asked an assistant stage manager.

"Mr. Hartog wants them in there," said the man. "He feels their presence helps the rehearsals and is thinking of turning them loose on stage."

Once Gurney recovered from his fright, he began to see what the director was up to. And he agreed it would be a bold idea to have the bloodthirsty hounds in full view throughout the performance. The device would keep the audience tense, never knowing whether the rottweilers might break loose and tear people in the front rows to pieces—a neat way to keep viewers totally involved.

Each member of the tight-knit cast pitched in with a will, totally embracing the life of his or her role. In the final week of rehearsal, two minor players, cast as homicide dicks, were picked up by Broadway police for yanking a derelict into a deserted alley and working him over until he was close to death. Clement Hartog thought he would see what he could do to arrange for their release, but Philip Undertag had already interceded, using his influence to get the charges dropped. When they turned up at rehearsals the next day, the cast cheered them lustily.

It surprised Gurney that they were completely remorseless.

"I'd do it again," said one of them. "The cocksucker mouthed off to us in public."

"I'd like to know what happened to respect for the badge," said the other with a look of disgust.

"It's all right," said Hartog softly, speculatively. " I don't know if I would have gone as far as you fellows did, but I fully approve. I like that in an actor. It's good for the show."

Loving the rehearsals as he did, Gurney wished they could continue forever. But the out-of-town opening date rushed toward them as though it was an express train and they were strapped to the tracks.

The approaching date stimulated the cast, making them so unruly and violent they virtually foamed at the mouth. But it bothered Clement Hartog.

"I just wish we had more time," he said. "With breathing room, I always felt I could do anything."

Prior to the Broadway opening, there were to be two out-of-town tryout cities—the first, Winslow in the Pacific Northwest, and the second the larger town of Holliman in one of the Southern border states. Hartog much preferred the traditional tryout cities of Boston, New Haven, and Philadelphia, trusting the critics in these venues, who were tough but fair, and whose comments could be useful in gearing a show for its Broadway opening. He was frankly baffled by the Undertag office's choice of the little-known cities in far-flung parts of the United States.

"Don't sell Winslow and Holliman short," said Undertag. "I'll concede that the theatre is a little foreign to Winslow. But Holliman has real roots in drama and some awfully sound critics who understand the growing pains of an incoming musical. Not only that, but Winslow has a university nearby, and both have fine little subscription lists that will help us make back all that money I'm laying out."

Undertag then admitted that the incoming-show traffic had tied up the three major tryout towns and that he simply could not get *Violencia* booked into them.

"But I'm far from displeased with Winslow and Holliman."

Hartog was upset by these choices, but not devastated.

"Finally," he said, "an audience is an audience. Our show is a little special, but if you've got something going for you, you can kill them in either Paris or Toledo. Actually, I'm more concerned about the show itself. I feel we're underrehearsed and a good week behind schedule. It's a bloody crime to be opening in this condition."

"I agree with you on that," said Norman Welles. "Why don't we grab Undertag by the neck and get the little sonofabitch to postpone for a week? We need every possible advantage for the show and for my songs to realize their full potential."

They checked with Mr. Mortimer, who said it would cost the producers a fortune to postpone.

"But I think you fellows are going to be surprised at the way your show pulls together," he said with a pixieish grin.

Mr. Mortimer had done more shows than anyone could count. Thus, even Hartog was heartened by his attitude. But Welles still insisted they fight for more time.

"My numbers are so underdrilled it's pathetic. And I'm positive I'm going to be destroyed in the notices. I've never taken a show on the road in this kind of shape."

But Clement Hartog seemed defeated and lacked the heart for this particular battle.

The night before he left for Winslow, Gurney had a sad farewell dinner with Angela, who accepted the news of his departure without a murmur. She simply lowered her great eyes and kissed him good-bye. At times he wished she would give him more of a fight on things. Gilda Gurney would have made him feel awful about leaving and not taking her along, even though he was making the trip for his work, which demanded total monklike concentration. He was not used to Angela's gentle and submissive ways, and could not get over his good fortune in having teamed up with her. But he had a way of sabotaging terrific situations, and he felt confident he would find a way to undermine this one, too.

For the trip out to Winslow, Gurney, in an extravagant mood, rented a large car that fell just short of being a limousine. He felt carefree and heady as he hit the road; it was the first time he had ever taken a trip and left nothing of importance behind. There was Angela, of course, but their future was far from being firm. And he could always call and ask her to shoot out for a visit.

Aside from Angela, there was really nothing—no home in particular, no kids, no job at the Bureau. For all anyone cared, he might just as well remain in Winslow; no one would know the difference.

He took the tricky-bodied chorus girl, Holly, and her Indian roommate along for company. Nothing much happened on the road, the girls sleeping in a separate cabin when they stopped over at motels. Gurney figured that Holly simply wanted to take her time and be discreet, not tip off her roommate about the strength of her feelings for him. In truth, Gurney didn't particularly lust after Holly, although he wouldn't have minded a brief tumble or two with the comely dancer. Actually, he was a little concerned about that tricky body of hers, perhaps afraid that he might get tied up in one of her contortions.

At a filling station about halfway along in the trip, Holly's Indian roommate, who had been pushing for a speaking part in the show, took Gurney aside.

"You know," she said with a mischievous twinkle, "Holly and I do 'sandwiches.'"

"Thanks, Jhumpa," Gurney had said, "but I'm not hungry at the moment."

It was only later, when they'd arrived in Winslow, that Gurney realized he'd been given an invitation to three-way sex. And he certainly would not have minded being in that type of sandwich.

Just as Clement Hartog suspected, Winslow proved to be a curious choice for an out-of-town opening. The streets of the small town were almost deserted and the city had a barren windswept look—as though whatever might have been there had been swept farther west by a storm. Gurney dropped the chorus kids off at the motel that had been reserved for them and then drove to his own hotel, which was in the center of town. It was a huge, shambling building that seemed out of place in tiny Winslow. Its lobby was somewhat deserted, too, causing Gurney to wonder if he had been the first one to arrive. He had a hard time getting the desk clerk's attention, ringing his head off until she finally appeared, a scholarly-looking woman with her hair in tight ringlets and a perfect square of a grin on her face.

"You're Mr. Gurney, of course," she said. "You'll probably want these."

She handed him some advance clippings related to the show that had evidently been published in the local newspaper. One had a picture of Gurney, which he felt was a good likeness, except for the goatee. This was curious, since he had not worn one for many years. He'd had the minibeard in college and shaved it off, just before applying for a job at Homicide.

Gurney thanked the woman, who summoned a quartet of bellhops—a captain and three assistants, to be precise. Gurney did not feel he needed all those bellhops for his one small suitcase, but he thought perhaps it was the custom for writers of tryout shows to have that many—so he allowed them all to help him, handing one an umbrella, another his newspaper, and a third a bag of potato chips he'd bought along the way.

"I hope you enjoy your stay with us," the desk clerk said as Gurney was leaving, "and that your show isn't a flop."

A suite of rooms had been prepared for him. It was nowhere near as lavish as his quarters in Beverly Hills, but it had much more room than he required, all the same. There was very little furniture in the suite, however. Gurney could not figure out whether the monster hotel was still being built or was being torn down. He called Clement Hartog, who said he had checked in many hours before and had been trying all the while to get room service, but to no avail.

"I have a feeling that another director would be able to convey, on the phone, just how important he is—and be able to get whatever it is he wanted in no time. I would feel awkward doing that, Paul. What do I say, that I am Clement Hartog, director of dozens of first-rate films and shows and that I insist on having some aspirins straightaway? How would that sound? And what would it mean in Winslow?"

Gurney said that he would be happy to call room service on Hartog's behalf and to lay out his powerful credentials, but the director insisted it wasn't necessary. He then told Gurney that the most thrilling part of doing a musical, any musical, was coming up in an hour.

"We will all congregate and hear the song orchestrations for the first time. Ty Sabatini has been up here for three days working with the twenty-seven musicians. He's assembled the finest people in the Winslow area—and I know, I know, that's a big laugh. But he says that frankly they're not all that bad. In any event, I want you to be there, Paul, along with the full cast, to hear them strike up that first note. If it doesn't give you goose bumps, I miss my guess. That one moment is probably why we are all in show business."

"I wouldn't miss it for the world, Clement."

Gurney unpacked, looked around, and speculated for a moment on what it would be like to have a party for selected members of the chorus, one that might, with luck, casually turn into an orgy. He imagined it concluding with him twisted up in one of Holly's contortions, maybe with Jhumpa thrown in as a sexual hors d'oeuvre. And he would get to have his sandwich after all.

The drive had made him sleepy, and he decided to take a little nap. Working preposterously long hours in Homicide, he had developed the knack of taking small, parceled-out dozes, setting his mind like a clock so that he could wake up whenever he wanted to, right on the dot. He hopped onto the bed and fell asleep immediately.

When he awoke, much later, he knew instantly that the technique had failed him for the first time—and that he was in major trouble.

It was almost dark; the streetlamps below had already been turned on, giving the seemingly deserted town a harsh, bitter light of the kind that might have been used for Essie Hartog's Berlin productions. He could imagine actors in black turtlenecks flashing through the streets, inveighing against the social forces that had yanked them prematurely from their mothers' wombs.

Gurney had forgotten—or perhaps he never knew—where the orchestra rehearsals were being held. He tore through the empty streets, onto one and out the other, until he finally came to a large barnlike affair, the only structure in the town that seemed big enough to hold an orchestra. He went inside and saw quickly that it was a Jewish center—and that he was in the wrong place.

As he raced through the streets again, he wondered why tiny Winslow had all those Jews. But then it made sense to him. Jews are known for their support of the theatre, another reason Undertag had selected the town.

About to abandon hope, he circled the town once again; finally, he heard orchestral sounds coming from the second floor of what appeared to be a deserted department store. Speeding through a ghostly ready-to-wear section, he found a stairway and burst into the orchestra room, just as the first notes of the second-act finale were being struck. Sabatini stopped the orchestra.

"Willkommen to our author," he announced, "who is a little late, n'est-ce pas? Andante, formaggio, fortissimo, fuckerooney."

Gurney guessed that Sabatini was annoyed because this was the first time he'd gotten to show off his wares; therefore, in his eyes, it was inexcusable for Gurney to turn up late. With his heart in his mouth, Gurney looked around until he saw Hartog, who refused to meet his eyes. The director simply shook his head in wonderment and disappointment. From the start, Gurney had disappointed the old man time after time. He hated himself for this.

The cast—*And God bless them all,* he thought—got him partially off the hook by applauding his appearance at length, and vigorously.

"Please, please," he said, holding up his hand, "I'm a terrible person. Let me at least feel awful for a while."

Sabatini continued on with the finale, a reprise of an earlier number called "My Kind of Dick" in which the young detective hero, played by Matt Tanker, sings the old Chief out of the Bureau. His message, essentially, is that "*My* Kind of Dick" is fair and has some social conscience while "*Your* Kind of Dick," which was once acceptable, is now bullshit and has to go.

Everything Hartog had said about the first orchestral note was true: It was thrilling. But it soon occurred to Gurney that this applied *only* to the first note. All that followed seemed saccharine, as though it were originating from the rooftop of a hotel in Cincinnati and being played over car radios.

Gurney tried to get his blood to surge, but to no avail.

Ty Sabatini, as a special concession to Gurney, doubled back over several of the songs the orchestra had already played; each of them had that same car radio/rooftop sound to them.

After the rehearsals, Gurney mentioned this to Norman Welles, who said the orchestrations had been done by a brilliant young fellow named Henry Stange who came highly recommended by composers who'd had hit shows with him.

"Do you agree with me on those sounds, though?" Gurney persisted.

"He has one of the finest reputations in the business," said Norman Welles. "And for Christ's sakes, he's young and he personifies everything that's happening in the theatre today."

When Gurney saw that he wasn't getting anywhere with Welles, he approached Clement Hartog and asked him *his* feelings about the arrangements.

"I know, I know," said the director, holding his head. "Don't get me sick."

Scene 9

G urney and Hartog had dinner at a nearby restaurant that
seemed amazingly continental for a farflung town like
Winslow. It was elegantly appointed, if a little funereal.
Gurney could not help but wonder who in the world frequented the
place in the barren, seemingly deserted town of Winslow.

The restaurant was called Sardi's Pacific Northwest. Hartog
and the owner seemed to be acquainted, although the director never
got around to explaining how he knew the fellow. The menu was
the largest and longest Gurney had ever seen, with a strong emphasis on seafood and rare and exotic Jewish cooking.

As Gurney was about to put in his order, Hartog leaned
across to him.

"Stick with the chicken," Hartog said. "It's the only safe
item on the menu."

"How do you know that?" asked Gurney.

"I know these places," said the director.

The owner, a gruff and burly Hungarian, came over and
presented them with little dishes of jelly beans, which struck Gurney
as being an odd sort of hors d'oeuvres. He took a seat beside them
and began to complain in a loud voice about how difficult it was to
get good help and about his terrible breakage problem.

Gurney thought it was a little rude of him not to inquire about *Violencia* and to wish them well. If the show caught fire, it certainly wasn't going to do the restaurant any harm.

Across the room, a young character actress who played an undercover dick in the show signaled to the owner and complained about having to wait more than an hour for her appetizer. He approached her table.

"You know who I worry about?" he said, slapping a drink from her hand. "My help, not you. You'll continue to wait."

Gurney and Hartog got up as one to intercede on her behalf, the director reaching the owner first.

"What are you doing?" he said. "She's just a kid."

As he stood by supportively, it was Gurney's feeling that the remark could have been a lot stronger.

"Let her go somewhere else if she don't like it," said the owner. "If I start losing my help, I'll be in some pickle. That's more important to me than some Broadway pisher."

When the owner stormed off, Gurney suggested they tell him to go fuck himself.

"Surely there's another place to eat," he said.

"Where might that be?" asked Hartog. "This, m'boy, is it."

"Well, I'd rather eat goddamned potato chips," said Gurney, but he was saying it for the benefit of the young character actress and knew he didn't mean it.

He sat down with Hartog, wanting in the worst way to tell him how sorry he was about missing the first thrilling note of the orchestra rehearsal, even though it wasn't that thrilling. But he could not convey this with any real conviction. Instead, he told the director he was willing to do whatever might be required, stay up all night if necessary, to sharpen and refine the libretto of *Violencia*.

"It's a little late for that," said Hartog, generously covering Gurney's hand with his own.

Several precious days remained for technical and dress rehearsals. Then, come hell or high water, they would open.

"And it's that opening that troubles me," said Hartog. "You might say, 'Well, we're buried way out here in Winslow, a real toilet, so what does it matter? We're getting ourselves prepared for New York and New York only.' But it doesn't work that way. Watch and see who shows up, and I'm not just talking about critics. Everyone in the theatre who either hates us or has reason to be jealous of Essie and me will be here, don't you kid yourself. To us, it will be just another rehearsal, but the vultures won't take that into consideration. They'll go back east and spread the word that we're a turkey."

"Would they travel this far to do something that nasty?" asked Gurney.

"They'd go to the moon for a little treat like that," Hartog said with a bitter laugh.

When the two had finished their main courses, Mr. Mortimer arrived, out of breath, his hands raised as though he had soaked them and was hanging them out to dry.

"You'd better come quickly," he said. "Mr. Welles has just been poisoned and needs to see you."

Hartog and Gurney signed for their meals quickly and then dashed up to Welles' suite, where they found the composer in bed, doubled over in agony. He said that he had eaten the Sardi's Pacific Northwest cotellettes á la Kiev, with side helpings of blini, sour cream, and a double order of shashlik.

"And then I felt a mysterious sharp pain in my side."

Hartog apologized for not having gotten to him before dinner and warning him against anything other than the chicken. Gurney was amazed that Norman Welles, who was so health-conscious and took such good care of himself, would order an exotic and risky dish in a strange off-the-path restaurant.

"Sometimes I fall off the trolley and think I can get away with it," said Welles, clutching his abdomen. "The only thing I hope is that this doesn't reduce the numbers of years I have left, even by a little bit. Everyone in my family has lived to be ridiculously old and I certainly don't want to be the first one to die young. And I probably will, too; I can see it coming. And after all the things I've done for myself."

Welles' food poisoning seemed to presage a series of setbacks for the company. The following day, one of the chorus people fell from the top of a Han Nihsu pagoda formation, broke his back, and had to be replaced by a local dancer who was nowhere in his league in terms of grace and precision of movement. And late that evening, Ty Sabatini got a wire from his wife that she had fallen in love with a cinematographer in Rome and planned to divorce the music conductor immediately upon his return. Sabatini, who was subject to severe depression anyway, really went into one this time and ended up going on one of the wildest binges that anyone in the company could recall.

But all of this paled beside the misfortune that hit the group midweek.

With the playing of a chord on the piano, Han Nihsu stopped the rehearsal one day to make the following announcement:

"It is my sad duty to inform everyone that Mr. Mortimer has been found hanging in the clothing closet of his suite at the Hotel Winslow."

Everyone was both shocked and sickened by the news. Clement Hartog, of course, canceled rehearsals for the rest of the day, even though there was precious little time to get the show in shape, the lost hours representing a big loss to the production.

Along with everyone else, Gurney felt awful about losing Mr. Mortimer, who had been a favorite of his; he could not drive the picture from his mind of the large, good-humored old teddy bear of a man hanging from a clothing closet hook. Later, over drinks, Han Nihsu said that Mr. Mortimer had left a note saying he was sick with remorse over a failed love affair with a young stagehand in a traveling company of *Uncle Vanya*. To compound the tragedy and to make everyone feel especially awful, Mr. Mortimer, before taking his life, had written out a detailed plan for the backstage handling of the props and sets for *Violencia*. Thus he had insured that it would be an easy matter for his assistant to carry on.

Despite these setbacks, the production somehow moved on. At the dress rehearsals, Rolf Rienzo's costumes were unveiled. As far as Gurney could tell, they displayed none of the medieval tapestried look that had gotten Rienzo his reputation. That possibility had concerned Hartog. But the designer had elected to give the costumes a burnt orange theme; obviously, in dressing the criminals and dicks in the bizarre color, Rienzo had in mind some comment he wanted to make on law enforcement. But even before Gurney could venture an opinion, Clement Hartog was at the designer's side, patiently explaining that his intentions were perhaps a bit too subtle for what he described as "the audience of today."

"Would it be possible, Rolf," he asked, "to tone down that orangy look before the opening?"

Asked to deal with a request of that nature, the Rolf Rienzo of old might have quietly gone off to slash his wrists—but he seemed to have made a good recovery from his depressive ten-year illness.

"I'll do it, Clement," said the designer, "but I'll have to come down gradually, one shade at a time."

Bess Filimino's sets presented yet another difficulty. Each one was minimal, but impeccably chosen. A single pair of handcuffs suggested—with some success—the entire detective bullpen; a pair of bloodstained panties represented, with perhaps more power than a stageful of props, the microanalysis department. The entire settings of *Violencia* could easily have fit into a small boy's summer camp trunk; yet the very delicacy of these sets made for difficult handling. Each had to be glided into place on strings and runners that would be invisible to the audience. The process required immaculate handling and enormous patience on the part of the harried stage crew. Sadly enough, there was no experienced Mr. Mortimer on hand to see that the procedure ran smoothly.

Throughout this period, Gurney felt curiously helpless. For some reason, he had pictured the week in Winslow as an opportunity for riotous carryings-on, but as it turned out, the cast was either too busy or too tired to do much partying. Gurney spent a great deal of time as a solitary drinker in his hotel suite. Moving back and forth from his quarters was no easy business, either, since, for some reason, the hotel had posted flat-faced, heavy-shouldered security guards in plain clothes on each floor and at strategic points along the lobby. Each time he tried to enter the elevator, Gurney was forced to show his credentials.

Annoyed by this nuisance, he complained one night to a guard, who responded in an ominous tone.

"We run a nice family place here."

"Now look," said Gurney, "I've worked around dicks for years."

"Really?" said the guard. "You'll have to tell me about it sometime."

Once Welles had recovered from his abdominal pains, Gurney, to vary his routine, had breakfast with the composer in his suite several times.

One morning, Welles ushered him in excitedly and said: "I just got word from Tippy, who is trusted by them, that the chorus kids are smoking dope and fucking each other's brains out. That's why they look so exhausted every morning, and believe me, we're going to pay for this once we open. Holly, the one you're crazy about, takes on all four of Han Nihsu's assistants every night in wild sexual bouts, getting into odd postures for them, which they love and know how to handle. Her friend Jhumpa is involved in something called 'sandwiches.' I think we ought to do something about it, don't you?"

"What can we do?" said Gurney, who realized he had lost his appetite.

Later in the day, Gurney studied the chorus kids carefully during rehearsals; it might have been his imagination, but it struck him that they were yawning an awful lot and that their eyes had a glazed and sexually sated look to them. He had the feeling that Welles' information was probably accurate. What was awful was that he knew of no way to shoehorn himself into the orgies.

During a five-minute break, he interrupted Holly, who was doing an extravagant back bend; designed to loosen up the muscles, it had the side effect of being maddeningly erotic. He asked her how she felt about having a drink with him after rehearsals.

"You couldn't possibly be serious," she said. "I like you, Mr. Gurney, and you're cute, but I am *so* exhausted."

"I'll bet you are," Gurney muttered to himself—and thought he heard a thin Far Eastern snicker from one of Han Nihsu's assistants. But when he wheeled around there was no one there.

Late that night, overcome with loneliness, he went for a walk through the barren streets of Winslow, stopping at a drugstore to page through some magazines.

"You a dick?" asked the propietor as Gurney flicked through a month-old copy of *Business Week*.

Gurney had to chuckle over the question, but instead of detailing his background in homicide—something he generally enjoyed doing—he simply said no, he wasn't.

"Then check these out," said the man, handing Gurney a stack of magazines featuring naked Danish girls in frenzied sexual postures. Gurney leafed through them, selected a few for purchase, and, for fun, tossed in a copy of *Anal Bike Messengers*. As he reached for his billfold, he looked back over his shoulder and became aware of someone staring at him. Spinning around quickly, he saw that it was the brilliantly quirky Hobie Hancock. Somewhat embarrassed, he stuffed the erotic puchases into a brown bag along with the lively information-packed business weekly.

"How much do I owe you for *Business Week?*" he asked, winking at the propietor to indicate he didn't want it known he was taking a bundle of pornography back to the hotel. Gurney's face was stiff as he walked along the street with Hancock and tried to make small talk. To his credit, the gifted young performer did not comment on Gurney's purchases, but focused instead on his own yearnings and future in the theatre.

"I would have thought it impossible, but the work on *Violencia* has been not only stimulating but also helpful to my budding career. We live and learn, n'est-ce pas?"

Gurney barely heard a word he said. He was convinced that Hancock knew about the bagful of porn and that it was a substitute for a real woman, Gurney being unable to produce one, even though he was the *writer* of the show and should have been able to come up with several at a snap of his fingers. For all of his discretion of the moment, the actor, Gurney felt, could probably hardly wait to rush back and unmask the librettist as a lonely hotel-room masturbator. Could the show possibly be a hit with such an unfortunate at the controls? He almost came out and asked Hancock to please not say anything, but he could not bring himself to do this. Instead, he excused himself and went upstairs to his room to call Angela.

"I need you to get on a plane and fly to Winslow as soon as possible," he told her. "It's vitally important."

Angela had a quiet, capable, unflashy style of getting things done. Without fanfare, she arranged to get to Winslow in no time flat. Gurney was coming along the corridor, outside his hotel suite, when he saw her being manhandled by one of the security guards. He walked over briskly, deliberately not running, knowing that if he got there too quickly he might kill the man. Taking the guard's wrist in a tight vise, and keeping his voice measured—something he'd trained himself to do, no matter what the provocation—he said: "Take your hands off her."

The guard directed a neutral, clear-eyed law enforcement look at Gurney that might have been unnerving had he not worked in the homicide field and seen it many times before.

"She's been claiming she belongs in one of the suites."

"She's with me," said Gurney, returning his own version of the look.

"I didn't realize she was your wife, Mr. Gurney. We go out of our way to protect spouses."

"She is my wife, sort of," said Gurney. "What's important is that I'm taking her with me."

"We try to do a decent job," said the man, bringing his jaw an inch from Gurney's.

"Then for God's sakes, do it," said Gurney, shoving the man aside and leading Angela to his suite.

Before opening the door, he whispered back to the man: "Can't you see she has a missing wing?"

Inside the suite, he hugged Angela as hard as he could, trying to squeeze all the loneliness out of himself. As if to demonstrate that she had a life and ideas of her own—and possibly influenced by her brush with security—she drew away from him and began to expound on the plight of America's student anarchists.

"The young intellectual has no channel for his energies, Paul, and this will inevitably lead to an explosion of the student elite."

She pranced around the room as she threw off her new ideas, her chest thrown out proudly. It was an Angela he hadn't seen before, and he enjoyed seeing this side of her. Everything about her was modest at a first glance, but improved on closer scrutiny. That was true of her jewelry, her clothing, her perfume, her features. After she had held forth for ten minutes or so on the intellectual frustration of the student radical, she sat down on the bed, shoulders slumped and out of breath.

"How's the show going?" she asked.

Gurney told her he couldn't say exactly, but that he had asked her to fly out to Winslow because, quite frankly, it was tedious hanging around theatre people. It wasn't quite true—he hadn't been hanging out with *anyone*—but it got him past the moment. As if exhausted by her sudden intellectual pursuits, she sighed and lay back on the bed. She was wearing a short flowered skirt that somehow tied in with her student-radical concerns. It fell back over her long tanned legs, and there was the fabled and careless glimpse of white panties, the effect of which was to make him pounce on her as if he'd been shot out of a gun. He made love to her as if he'd received word that it was the last time he'd be permitted to make love to anyone. Her style in bed—when he allowed her to have one—was never to let Gurney do anything to her unless she countered by offering some delicious treat of her own. When he came a second time—a famous first for him—her response was a low, gratified chuckle that had a note of gentle triumph to it.

Clement Hartog came by a bit later. Before admitting him, Gurney sealed Angela into one of the rooms and received the director in another—wondering all the while why he needed to go through with this deception.

"Got anybody in there?" Hartog asked, nodding toward the second room.

"Sort of," said Gurney.

"Someone in the show?" asked Hartog as if he were a teacher querying a naughty student. "If so, which one?"

Gurney thought the director was being much too nosy, but all the same he said: "Oh, for Christ's sakes, why lie, it's Angela. Come on out."

She appeared, trailing a blanket to cover her nudity, kissed Hartog on the cheek, and then went back to the other room so that the collaborators could either talk or work.

"I remember Angela," said Hartog. "How come you were keeping her under wraps?"

"Damned if I know," said Gurney. "I guess I felt that if we were going to work, I'd feel uneasy about having a girl in the next room."

"I know what you mean," said Hartog. "How could you really throw yourself into it? She's got a great body, incidentally, with a powerful little ass. But it's hard to concentrate that way. It's bad enough for me having Essie in the next room, and as you well know, she's just my mother."

As it turned out, Hartog didn't want to work at all, just to talk and relax for a bit. Gurney saw the visit as an opportunity to gauge the director's feelings about the shape they were in and their chances for becoming a hit.

Hartog was direct and concise.

"I don't think we're ready. We're not going to be ready in Winslow and I doubt we'll be ready in Holliman."

He sat there grimly, as though he were about to get a haircut from an untrustworthy barber.

"I wouldn't stake my life on it," he said, "but there's a small chance we'll be ready in New York."

Scene 10

On the morning of the opening in Winslow, Gurney walked over to check the theatre once again. Standing alone in the vast open space, aware that his pose was slightly dramatic, he took a rough count of the seats and saw that there were close to two thousand of them.

How in the world will we be able to pack the place, he wondered, *way out in Winslow?*

He had seen very few people in the tiny, windswept town and could not imagine Winslow having two thousand *residents,* much less theatregoers. But he'd heard there was a busy suburb just outside the town. Maybe that was where the potential audience resided.

By early evening, the center of Winslow had begun to bustle with traffic. Gurney's hotel, too, livened up considerably, as though a major convention were being held there. As it happened, there *was* such an event, a gathering of radiology equipment people.

Gurney had no idea if the radiology execs were coming to the opening of *Violencia.* He had mixed feelings about the possibility. On the one hand, they seemed an odd audience for a Broadway-bound musical; still, there were quite a few of them, they were not as badly dressed as some conventioneers he had seen—and they certainly would fill up the place. On the way back to his suite, Gurney saw one of them, who was not quite as drunk as he pretended to be, waving a foot-long vibrator at passing couples and winking as he did so.

"You'll never guess what *this* is for," he called out after them.

Despite the tasteless exhibition, Gurney felt sorry for the poor man. At the same time, he wondered why the normally alert security guards hadn't noticed him. They'd certainly kept a close eye on everyone else.

Gurney and Angela had a preopening light bite at Sardi's Pacific Northwest. The owner, completely oblivious to the importance of the occasion, was sunk deep in his own difficulties.

"I lost two cooks this morning," he moaned, "and the salad man just threatened to quit."

He didn't even offer the couple a good-luck drink, which Gurney felt was shabby treatment indeed—especially since the restaurant was now packed with people who were either *Violencia* opening-night guests or radiology specialists. *On how many other nights of the year does he get this much business?* Gurney wondered.

Diners, who looked suspiciously like East Coast theatre people, started to file past the table. Gurney did not know any of them personally, but Hartog, who had joined the couple, seemed to be acquainted with them all. As each one passed, the director would duck his head down beneath the table.

"Oh no, oh God no, not him. He's here for only one purpose—to run back with the news that we're a turkey."

Gurney was feeling like an outsider until he saw John Gable, the dick who had taken over his *Homicider* column and who had apparently, and amazingly, made the trip out to catch the opening of *Violencia*. Gable, who obviously felt out of his depth among all the veteran theatre people, did not approach their table, but did give Gurney and Angela a good-luck wave before slipping behind a counter in the rear of the restaurant and trying to be as inconspicuous as posssible. Gurney understood Gable's feelings. Just five or six months back, he might have behaved the same way. The man was a good, clear thinker, and Gurney was thrilled to see him. Not only did he now have a friend in Winslow, but Gable, as a homicider himself, might be able to furnish him with some useful tips after he had seen the production.

Gurney did not know the protocol for opening night. Did one send a telegram to each member of the cast? Flowers to the chorus kids? He decided he would send everyone an expensive gift for the New York opening, but to keep it down here to flowers for the two leads, Essie Hartog and Matt Tanker. He was completely baffled as to what to get for the gifted Hobie Hancock, finally settling on a magazine subscription to a well-known entertainment monthly, one that featured news about opportunities in show business for up-and-coming young performers.

He then paid a backstage visit to Essie Hartog. The aging actress's eyes were filmed over with a mixture of tears and excitement, and she might not have been aware of it when Gurney wished her the best. Matt Tanker's mother had been hired as her backstage dresser. She was busy oiling Essie Hartog's stilts and seemed to be in a rage because a famous doctor had said publicly that cancer might be emotionally induced.

"Can you imagine," she said, "a man like that, with all the good things he's done in his life, coming right out and saying something filthy like that? Shouldn't he think twice before he shoots his mouth off? They ought to take him out and give *him* cancer and see what kind of emotions he has."

Gurney did not agree at all. He felt it was much too rough a penalty to give a man for advancing a sincerely felt opinion. But since it was opening night, he did not stop to argue the point. Added to this, it seemed a strange sort of debate to be having before the premiere of a new show.

Gurney found Matt Tanker in an entirely different state from that of the Viennese actress. The ex-dick seemed calm, level-eyed, and peaceful as he sat on the floor of his dressing room, wearing a poncho and molding pottery pieces. He had come a long way from the days when he was a hard-nosed sex patroller—and he had even put some distance between himself and his more recent career as a highly paid L.A. chiropractor specializing in the injured backs of highway accident victims.

"It's a show," said Tanker with a curious, beatific little smile. "If it works out, fine. If not, I'll go up north to the mountains, find myself a cave, and investigate my head."

Try as he might, Gurney could not altogether admire Tanker's unruffled state of mind. Wasn't the actor being a bit smug, considering the fact that a small fortune was at stake, along with the careers of more than a hundred people? Was it possible that the actor was using dangerous hallucinogenic drugs? If so, it certainly wasn't going to help his line deliveries in the crucially important role of Essie Hartog's detective son. Gurney would have preferred that the male lead in *Violencia* be just a little bit keyed up. On the other hand, he had to ask himself what exactly was so great about his own contribution.

On the way back to his seat, Gurney took a quick look into the shabbily appointed chorus kids' dressing room and saw Han Nihsu's four assistants tossing the nimble-bodied Holly up in the air on a fireman's circular tarpaulin. They stopped immediately when they saw Gurney, who thought it was a peculiar warm-up exercise for the opening.

He took his seat then, alongside Angela, and thumbed through the show program. There was a bearded picture of him on the back page, along with the following notes:

"Librettist Paul Gurney, 39, is an ex-cop who has never done a show before. This is his first one, repeat, the first show he has ever done. He has no experience in the drama whatsoever, which is quite something when you think about it. Such are the vagaries of what we know as theatre in America. Gurney lives alone in an East Coast city and collects so-called 'art' pictures of naked young Danish girls."

Gurney was outraged by the final sentence. Evidently Hobie Hancock had gotten in touch with Nettie Hersel, the public relations woman who prepared the program notes, and told her about his onetime purchase of the hot magazines. It was bad enough for the actor to have ratted him out. For that idiot PR woman to so nakedly expose him . . .

Angela did her best to calm him down.

"It's only Winslow," she said. "And there's plenty of time for a correction before we get to New York."

She assured him that they might even be able to make some editorial changes before the show hit Holliman. Gurney gradually took control of himself and turned around to check the audience in the theatre, which was quickly filling to capacity. It looked about the way he imagined it would: A good many of the radiology people were there, along with a large contingent of well-dressed people he guessed were from the East Coast theatre world. There was another rather plainly dressed group that Gurney took to be the local Winslow crowd. The students did not seem to have shown up in any number, but there were two surprise contingents in the audience. One was made up of hotel security guards, who were scattered about and perhaps recognizable only to Gurney. He had no idea if they were there for security purposes or because they loved show business. But they seemed to be in a much jollier mood than they ever were when on duty—and since this was the case, he was rather glad they had turned up. Another group, which he did not know how to take at all, was a large body of seamen, some in dress uniforms, others in underwater wet suits. Hartog, coming over to wish his partner well, explained that they were from the local Underwater Demolition School and had been let in free as a courtesy gesture and to help fill up the house.

"They will laugh at the sexy stuff," said Hartog. "I've had them at openings before and you can count on it. I don't believe they can hurt us."

"And good luck to you, Paul," said Hartog, who then returned to his seat.

Just before the curtain went up, a fellow approached and introduced himself as Norbert Tiomkins, a classmate of Gurney's in grade school. Though Tiomkins had put on a great deal of weight, particularly in the jowls, Gurney recognized his old school chum immediately.

"We live out here in Winslow, Paul," said Tiomkins, "and we've been watching your every move with enormous pride. I wonder if you would join Maggie and me for a drink after the show?"

"Normally, I'd love to," said Gurney. "But I have a feeling my collaborators and I are going to have our hands full after the opening and will have to have an immediate meeting. Perhaps some other time, Norbert."

"Not on your life," said Tiomkins, who evidently had not been prepared for a turndown. His jowls shook with rage. "My wife and I wouldn't shit on the best part of you and your wife."

He then scooped up a woman Gurney took to be Mrs. Tiomkins and stormed out of the theatre. Gurney then realized that his own response had been a bit on the smug side, however honest in its intentions—and that perhaps Tiomkins's reaction was not as inappropriate as it first seemed.

The reference to Angela as Gurney's wife made the librettist slink down in his seat, almost reflexively, as though his ex might at any moment come in and spot the two of them. How preposterous that was, Gurney thought, straightening his back. For one thing, she was his *ex*-wife, and he could certainly go to the theatre with anyone he liked. Added to this, it would not surprise him in the least if Gilda Gurney was rolling around on a carpet somewhere with a treacherous colleague they'd met together at one of the Homicide family picnics.

As the bland overture began, the new stage manager, who had taken over for the deceased Mr. Mortimer, presented Gurney with what seemed to be a ticket-purchasing bill. Studying it quickly, Gurney saw that he was being asked to pay for the choice orchestra seats of the eighteen hotel security guards.

"This is outrageous," said Gurney. "I didn't invite them."

The fellow used the lame excuse that he was "just following orders," then added, "And it has to be paid or the curtain can't go up."

Was it possible that the security guards had discovered that Gurney was an ex-homicider and assumed that, as a courtesy, he would want them to attend the show as his guests? If that was so, it was a law enforcement custom Gurney had never heard of, and he thought he was familiar with all of them.

"I'll have to make out a check," said Gurney. "But I'm going to look into this and will probably insist on getting my money back."

The curtain finally went up on one of Bess Filimino's tiny but exquisitely made sets. Gurney, who had expected to be limp with nervous tension, found that he was surprisingly calm about the experience. He was able to sit back and watch the show just as if he were a normal audience person. And in a sense he was, since he had never really seen *Violencia* run straight through, with no interruptions from either Clement Hartog or the technical staff. Or perhaps his nonchalance derived from that cynical side of himself which remained aloof from show business, even though he was in the thick of it.

When the audience applauded Essie Hartog's first appearance, she answered them with a loud, vulgar farting sound, an old good-luck custom from her Berlin theatre days, one that most of the people in the audience did not quite comprehend. The underwater demolition people razzed back at her, some of them turning and farting in the direction of the stage, evidently thinking it was a new kind of audience-participation show. No question, their raucousness, though in answer to Essie's vulgarity, did tend to dilute the effect of the opening number—for which Welles, without consulting his collaborators, had infuriatingly switched the lyrics around, so that the chorus once again confusingly sang "I Love Paris in the Off-Season" instead of the agreed-upon "I Love Precinct Nineteen in the Off-Season."

In spite of the bumpy start, the audience quickly settled down and seemed to enjoy the first fifteen minutes of the show. A turning point came during Betty Pound's wistful "I Can't Get His Gun Off" number, which the theatregoers perhaps misinterpreted as being salacious in its intentions. Shaking her hips as she did and using some of the buttock manipulations Han Nihsu had supplied her with, the scrappy, zesty little one-armed actress did nothing to reduce this impression and rather helped it along. The underwater demolition crowd in particular gave her a good working-over, shouting out obscene catcalls and many of them passing notes up to the stage with invitations for meetings after the show.

Neophyte librettist though he was, Gurney could not help but detect some restlessness in the audience. He felt strongly that the show had lost a great deal of their sympathy and goodwill for a major part of the first act. Not until the act finale, when Hobie Hancock was dragged in and chained to a radiator, some of the dicks going after him with bone-bangers, other more socially enlightened ones trying to restrain their colleagues, (at least until they had a feasible explanation as to why he'd slaughtered so many pants-pressers), did Gurney feel a current of excitement return to the show. Though the applause was far from tumultuous, it was decent enough, much of it coming from the contingent of hotel security guards. It turned out to be a stroke of luck that they'd been invited. He decided he would let his check clear and say no more to anyone about it.

During the intermission, Gurney, with Angela coming along beside him, sought out Clement Hartog in the rear of the theatre. He was in a state of frustration when they found him.

"We had 'em," he said, "and then we lost 'em."

"I'll tell you what's strange," said Undertag, who had flown west at the last minute and was unable to get a seat. "The audience wants to like this show. And you folks aren't letting 'em.

"They ask for so very little," he continued, an odd whimper coming into his voice. "Why would you want to not give it to them?"

"I believe we'll give it to them in the second act," said Hartog. "We've been doling it out. . . ."

"So that they really appreciate it when they get it," said Gurney, once again rallying to the support of his director.

Toileau joined the group, looking more dapper than ever and quite aloof.

"I see you've gone ahead and kept 'doody,'" he said.

There was a good deal of hurt in his tone. Gurney could only look down at the floor, avoiding the man's eyes.

Mandarin, who had come along with the producing team, took Gurney aside.

"There's so much there, Paul. Would that I had been given the opportunity to direct it. I think you would have seen your values realized."

Mandarin's naked and somewhat ruthless ambition always came wrapped in a coating of gentle concern. As a result, it invariably took Gurney by surprise and never offended him as much as it no doubt should have.

"I think Clement is doing a fine job," said Gurney. "Give him a chance. And don't forget, this is only Winslow."

The second act got off to a rousing, foot-tapping start, beginning, as it did, with the "Let Us Inform You of Your Constitutional Rights" number, sung by a quartet of dicks as they ironically smashed a suspect to a bloody pulp. Even Norman Welles' light romantic musical approach could not dampen the effect of the piece as it reached the final chorus. With the victim stretched out in the bullpen and beaten into insensibility, several of the hotel security guards in the audience advanced on the stage, shouting, "Bravo."

"You"d think they were seeing *South Pacific,*" said Angela.

But as the second act turned more complex, with the mass-murdering Hobie Hancock character turning out to be a political operative closely affiliated with the Associated Union of Dry Cleaning Workers, Gurney could sense a return of the first-act restlessness in the audience.

Halfway through the act, steam began to pour out into the theatre. It had a fragrant, not entirely unpleasant odor to it. Puzzled at first, Gurney soon realized that he was smelling overcooked shashlik from Sardi's Pacific Northwest, which bordered on the theatre. To verify this suspicion, Gurney looked around at Norman Welles' seat and saw that the composer had grown ashen, finally falling to the floor, where he once again began to writhe in agony. It was difficult to tell if this was caused by dissatisfaction with *Violencia* or by the restaurant's attempt at gourmet cooking. Whatever the case, several members of the audience left their seats and began to file out of the theatre. Perhaps given courage by the first walkouts, many more people got up and left, too, the small exodus soon becoming a stampede.

Gurney looked around and would have sworn that Norman Welles had been crushed underfoot by the young, vigorous underwater demolition people in their haste to vacate the theatre. Feeling that his actions were high-minded, Gurney remained gamely in his seat. Among the huffier walkouts was John Gable. Gurney would have sworn he'd stick it out to the last, if only as a courtesy gesture.

"You sure got a lot of guts, kid," he said as he passed Gurney's seat, and then joined the outgoing throng.

Gurney felt this was poor form on Gable's part, a real kick in the teeth. Still, he clung to the hope that his old colleague had actually enjoyed the show but was forced to leave because of the shashlik fumes.

By the time the curtain came down on the second and final act, only Gurney, Angela, Clement Hartog, and a cluster of hotel security guards were left seated in the theatre. The tiny band members gave the cast a big hand, trying to make as much noise as possible and insisting on two curtain calls. Clement Hartog, in a brave and moving gesture, laid a bouquet at his mother's stilts.

When the curtain came down the second time, Gurney walked over and put his arm around the forlorn director's shoulder.

"We had 'em again," said Hartog. "But this time around we lost 'em for good."

Norman Welles, bloody and trampled upon, looked bewildered.

"You guys may not know it, but we're in big trouble. I've never had this happen before. There wasn't one of my numbers that drew really big applause. Forgive me, Paul, and watch your temper, but the libretto wasn't any bargain, either. I may have to pull out. Not only that, but you fellows don't know these producers. They're liable to close the show before I even get to quit."

Essie Hartog, in her dressing gown, came out from the wings. It soon became clear that she was still hypnotized by the emotional impact of her return to the stage. As a result, she hadn't even realized that all but a handful of people in the audience had walked out of the show.

"They loved me," she said. "I knew they would and they did."

Clement Hartog came forward quickly and stroked his mother's hair.

"They more than loved you, darling," he said, "they adored you."

The three collaborators then took seats, each of them gloomily assessing the condition of *Violencia* and concluding that the prospects did not look good.

But then Philip Undertag came skipping down the aisle and surprised them.

"The show's a stinker in its present condition, but I don't think it's that difficult to fix."

It was entirely possible that the producer was speaking out of self-interest. After all, he had taken over the Pokerino and completely restructured it to meet the specific needs of *Violencia.* Apart from the embarrassment of a closing—though Lord knows he was a veteran in this area—he would have an empty theatre in the city, a situation that would cost him quite a bit of money. Whatever the case, the three collaborators could not help but be cheered by his attitude.

Even though they were all physically and emotionally drained by the experience, the group met at once in Undertag's suite. What the producer had in mind was a certain pruning out of the more conspicuously objectionable elements in the show.

"First off," he said with a nod toward the distinguished-looking Toileau, "we get rid of that 'doody' line."

Tolileau lowered his eyes in modest triumph.

Both Gurney and the director looked at Undertag with a mutually steady gaze. It had always been Hartog's view that if you let Philip Undertag talk, without interruption, he would begin to deflate as he gradually lost confidence. How much could he have, really, after all those years of consistent theatrical defeat. But this time, his assurance was reinforced by the thunderous rejection of a short while ago. He did not back up.

"The line is not doing us any good, and it may be harming us. You fellows probably noticed that the really big walkout came on 'doody.'"

"I thought it came on the shashlik smells," said Hartog innocently.

"I disagree," said Undertag. "I think shashlik started them on their way and then 'doody' clinched it. Whatever your feelings, you've got to agree that the 'doody' line isn't scoring for us and may be offending some people."

Hartog and Gurney were silent, neither agreeing nor disagreeing. Undertag went on. His thought was that if certain of what he considered the vulgar elements were excised, and a thread of wholesomeness laced in—very subtly—the show had a hell of a chance to make it.

"Can you give us some examples?" asked Hartog.

"Frankly, no," said Undertag. " You fellows are the creative ones. And I certainly don't want to change the basic nature of the show, which, as I understand it, is by design ballsy. I just think it can be made *fun* ballsy, that's all."

"And more theatrical," Toileau put in.

"What would happen, for example," said Undertag, "and I'm not pushing this, even though it is my money and my theatre . . . what would happen if the kid detective were to call the old Chief 'Daddy' a few times? Let's just speculate on that. Would the show really be injured? Would anything be fundamentally different? Think a second. Or let's say the dicks, instead of smashing Hancock over the head, lifted him to his feet once in a while and told him he's probably not a bad guy, but that they're just doing their job. 'Put yourself in our shoes,' they could say, and you know, Norman, that's not a bad idea for a song. You could write the hell out of a song like that."

"It'll never work," the composer said glumly. " And I'll get killed for your idea."

"All right, forget that. I never claimed to be creative. But would a touch like that, here and there, really hurt the show, fellas? In your heart of hearts, would it? Or let's say, at the end, instead of the young detective booting his old man out of the Bureau, the two of them went out for a cheeseburger. Would that kill you guys? I'm just saying that it just might do us a helluva lot of good. I'm trying to save the show, fellas, because there's a lot to like in it, and I want to bring the damned thing in."

Undertag's argument was not only a sincere one but, for all of its weakness, was frustratingly difficult to challenge—especially since he was quite believable when he said he liked *Violencia* and would do anything to save it.

"I know, I know, Philip," said Hartog in reply to the producer's suggestions, "but it's just not the show we wrote."

Gurney had the uneasy feeling that the director might have been a bit more conciliatory if he, the librettist, had not been present. But perhaps he wasn't being fair to Hartog.

A bit later, the two repaired to Gurney's suite, Angela darting into the other room when she sensed that they wanted to be alone.

"Don't worry, Paul," said Hartog. "We're not going to knuckle under. I'd rather close the show than alter the conception."

But the director's weary eyes seemed to be saying something else. Gurney tried to make it easier for him.

"Well now, Clement, were his suggestions really so preposterous?"

"That's just it," said Hartog, grabbing at the bait. "He may have had a thousand turkeys in a row, but he's not an entirely stupid man. Maybe he's on to something, even though he's not expressing himself brilliantly.

"Look, Paul," he continued, "there are changes we both want to make anyway. So let's really go at it. Between now and our opening in Holliman we can get a ton of work done. We'll keep Undertag's suggestions way in the back of our minds and at the same time vow not to change the basics of *Violencia,* even if our lives were to be put at stake. If we get him to push back the opening date in Holliman, we can bring in a show nobody will even recognize. And it will still be *Violencia.*"

"I'll drink to that," said Gurney.

And he did. The best part of the plan was that he would be getting back to work with Hartog, the two of them closeted for hours, having little snacks and exchanging boyhood anecdotes once again, even though there would be less time for that now.

There was a drawback, however. While it was true that they had succeeded in emptying a huge, packed theatre—whether it was the show or the shashlik—Gurney had really loved *Violencia*. It was rough and awkward, but it seemed to have a brutal, black-and-blue, malevolent growl of violence to it. The frightening picture of Essie Hartog on stilts, the accuracy of bloodstained homicidal panties, the bared fangs of chained-up police dogs—all of it struck him as being crudely correct. Despite its flaws, the show had an eerie, sour, whining, absolutely impeccable smell of the authentic to it. And now they were going to make it folksy. Or maybe they weren't. But they were going to change it, and this was painful for Paul Gurney to contemplate.

Though the reviews had not come in yet, Gurney, to lighten the atmosphere, recited a fictional one he felt might be written about the show:

SKIP THE SHOW, ORDER THE SHASHLIK
"Neither chained-up police dogs nor actresses on stilts nor great gusts of shashlik fumes wafting in from a neighboring restaurant, could disguise the fact that what transpired on the stage last night was essentially a small, tepid, quite dull and witless little concoction.

One can only wonder what outrageous whim on the part of the producers could have induced these chaps to feel that life in an uggghhh!!! homicide bureau might provide the materials for a quote Broadway entertainment. One's mind boggles at the thought of these presumably sane gentlemen investing yet one more cent in bringing this monument of dullness, this salute to insipidity, to the Great White Way. Yet latest information is that, indeed, that is their very plan. Well, good luck, gentlemen, good luck, and may reason, taste, and minimal intelligence soon return to all of us and to America."

Gurney, who had worked on the mock notice and wasn't really reciting it extemporaneously, caught the great director off guard. In all the time he had known him, he'd never heard Clement Hartog laugh quite that hard.

Yet, uncannily, the review in the morning *Winslow Standard* was an almost exact representation of Gurney's imagined one.

GOBBLE, GOBBLE, GOBBLE

"Neither real police dogs, nor second-rate actresses on stilts, nor a fading and desperate director's cutesy-pie idea of filling the Winslow theatre with shashlik fumes could disguise what was most apparent to the large group of unfortunates who assembled to view the soon-to-be-forgotten *Violencia* last night. This must surely go down (as quickly as possible, one would hope) as one of the most stupefyingly dull evenings in all theatrical history. . . ."

Gurney had an eerie feeling as Hartog read just about as much of the notice as he could stomach. It was almost as though the local critic had been under the bed taking notes, the night before. Indeed, Hartog suggested that perhaps he *had* been hiding under the bed.

"That happened to me once before, on a show I did in Harrisburg, Pennsylvania. We were goofing, the same way you and I were, and we caught the little fucker listening in through the window and taking notes."

The afternoon notice was not much kinder, although it put the emphasis on an assumption by the producer that the people of Winslow were unlettered no-nothings.

A SENSE OF SMELL

".... Do they think we're simps? Neanderthals? Well, we may not be sophisticated East Coast critics out here, but dammitall, we certainly know garbage when we see it—or shall I say smell it. And that's about the kindest comment I can make about the monstrosity that was foisted upon us last night, at—get this, kind sirs and mes-dames—$12.50 a ticket."

Without expressing their feelings aloud, both Gurney and Hartog had prayed for at least one nice word from Lester Daggo, the critic whose light, breezy capsule reviews appeared in a national entertainment monthly.

But Daggo, too, quickly took his place among the naysayers.

THANKSGIVING COMES EARLY

"The fact that *Violencia* is a turkey—and let me estab-lish quickly that it is most emphatically a bird of that nomenclature—could easily have been discerned by any-one fortunate—or shall we say, unfortunate—enough to be in on the show's beginnings. The frail and most un-appealing little creature was doomed from the start. I tried to tell the two young collaborators that, and nice young lads they are, too, but it was to no avail. They just kept plying deponent thine with club sandwiches and going about what turns out to be their not-so-merry way. Told ya, fellas." *Lester Daggo.*

"The creep," said Hartog. "He never said a word to us." The reviews, in a curious way, only served to anger Gur-

ney, who had always enjoyed being an underdog, the thrill of coming from behind. He had never actually pulled this off in his life, but
he could imagine what a treat it would be. And he was happy to
see that the various critical death sentences had the same effect on
Clement Hartog.

"It would really be wonderful to turn one of these things
around," said Gurney. "Really show these bastards. Ever see it happen, Clement?"

"Plenty of times," said the director. "And usually to my
shows. I can name you a dozen that weren't given a chance and that
came in as big hits. Guess what?"

"What's that?"

"It's going to happen to *Violencia*, Paul."

Scene 11

The first order of business was to put a little spark and hope into a cast that was, quite naturally, discouraged about the show's early reception. They could certainly have seen for themselves that the show wasn't clicking; it was no small accomplishment to drive almost two thousand people out of a theatre and could hardly be written off as a freak accident.

Hartog was brilliant in his handling of the dispirited team.

"I believe in *Violencia*," he said, "and I am not, at this stage of my career, about to let a handful of local yokels—local *putzes,* to put it in plain English, to influence me in the slightest."

Oh sure, Hartog conceded, the show had a way to go before it went over the top. But as far as he was concerned they all had another *Fiddler* on their hands. He may have been whistling in the dark, but Gurney could sense a lift in the spirits of the cast; he found himself cheering up as well. While *Violencia* finished up its Winslow run, Gurney and Hartog went at the show with a vengeance. Though it was no easy matter for him, Gurney sent Angela back to the East Coast. He felt awful as he waved good-bye to the slender, lovely, unselfish young woman, but he felt it was necessary; he wanted to be as unencumbered as possible for the big push. Some might have felt it would be a strength to have a perfect person around for support . . . but not Gurney.

Hartog and the ex-dick then tore into the libretto, often making decisions that might have seemed cruel to an outsider; it was apparent, for example, that Betty Pound, that double-barreled little bundle of dynamite and talent, just wasn't scoring in the show and had to be released. The feeling was that her role should go, too, along with her "I Can't Get His Gun Off" number, and this made the unpleasant task of releasing Betty Pound a little smoother. She fought hard, though, and did not make it easy on the director.

"Where do I go from here?" she asked. "How many parts come up in a season for a girl with one wing? Keep me in the show, Mr. Hartog, and I'll do anything from lowly chorus kid to wardrobe mistress. Only don't send me back east where I'm sure to have rough sledding."

Hartog wavered for a moment, but then decided that a clean break was best.

"It's for your own good, kid," he said softly, and then canned her.

Hartog then suggested that it was time to come down hard on Norman Welles and finally get him to alter some of his light love lyrics. The audience was obviously confused by numbers such as "Broadway Ragtime," which irritatingly accompanied a brutal grilling scene of an embittered assault and battery suspect. Welles, to everyone's frustration, put up a battle, but eventually gave in and made a few minor changes.

Hartog and Gurney then began to throw out numbers such as "Don't Blow Smoke Up My Ass" which just weren't paying off, and to substitute ones such as the upbeat "Bi Guys Can Be Nice Guys," to be sung by the Chief of the Vice Squad. Gurney did not fail to note that most of the changes were on the uplifting side and that, in some subtle way, there came about a certain incorporation of Undertag's ideas. In any event, by the time *Violencia* hit Holliman, it was an entirely different show, one that would have been only barely recognizable to anyone who'd remained to see the version that crashed and burned in Winslow.

If Winslow was lonely and windswept, Holliman, contrarily, was big and brimming with activity. Gurney's hotel was in the downtown area, close to the theatre, which protruded like a big toe from a boot-shaped area that was home to what appeared to be all of the underprivileged people in the city.

Gurney's hotel was dramatically different from the one he'd stayed at in Winslow, and he was glad of that, since *Violencia* was scheduled for a much longer run in Holliman. The service was of the highest order. So eager were the room service people to oblige that Gurney had to almost virtually beat them off with sticks. He was given a large suite once again, but this time around, it was a warmly furnished one with a terrace that looked out on the most attractive part of Holliman—a small port, lovely city lights, a view comparable to one that might have been visible from a flat overlooking New York City's East River. Gurney was so thrilled by the wonderful room service that soon after checking in, he began to order items that he didn't particularly want—just for the fun of it, and to get the taste of Winslow out of his mouth. The service people all seemed interested in the show, several of the bellhops whipping out manuscripts of plays they had written and asking for Gurney's professional opinion.

"You'd never believe it, fella," was his standard reply, "but I don't know much more about this field than you do."

The cast seemed to perk up noticeably as soon as they hit Holliman. They had turned a corner; the Winslow debacle was far behind them. As far as they were concerned they were in a brand-new show. Indeed, Philip Undertag sent a special letter to the Holliman drama critics telling them to pay no attention to the fact that *Violencia* had been called one of the great stinkers of all time in its previous incarnation. The show coming into Holliman was fresh off the assembly line.

"I have canned a great many of the people involved in the Winslow bomb," he said in his letter.

Gurney agreed with Hartog that this was defensive thinking and that it might have been more prudent not to have called attention to the show's early failings. But the letter did demonstrate a new outlook on the producers' part and a sign that they were willing to battle all the way down the line for *Violencia*.

The Holliman Theatre was strikingly modernistic; at the same time it had the look of a complicated chocolate cake that one might purchase in Switzerland. It was larger, if anything, than its Winslow counterpart. But in their efforts to make the interior interesting, the architects had placed at least a thousand of the seats either behind giant brown pillars or situated so that people assigned to them would have to twist themselves into tortured and gymnastic postures in order to see the stage.

Another negative feature was the acoustical arrangement. Norman Welles immediately pronounced it the worst he had ever encountered. Essie Hartog's bold and raucous voice, one of the genuine assets of the show, came across the footlights as a dying, faded crackle on a cheap transistor radio. The twenty-seven orchestra pieces, blaring away at their loudest, gave off a tiny humming sound that might have been produced by a child playing a comb. When the head sound man made an adjustment in his equipment, the theatre was filled with a thunderous whining sound that sent blood pouring from Ty Sabatini's nostrils.

"You can have one or the other," said the sound man, who along with the other Holliman backstage technicians was surly in his manner. "What'll it be?"

To his credit, Norman Welles, though still weakened from shashlik poisoning, spoke up boldly to the heavily muscled technician.

"Don't tell me I'm full of shit," he said. "That sound is awful. I've been in theatres ten times this size where my music has been heard by each person in the audience, with all of its charm and grace left fully intact."

Gurney stood ready to jump in and protect Welles if the sound man advanced toward him, but as it happened his help wasn't needed. Surprised by the onslaught from the thin-chested composer, the technician, who looked as though he could wipe out Welles by breathing on him, backed away.

"I'll see what I can do," he said meekly.

The one slightly ominous note on the horizon in Holliman was the posting of signs about the city announcing the arrival, for a speaking engagement, of an angry white supremacist, whose first "Hate Concert," as it was called, was scheduled for the very night that *Violencia* was to open. The demagogue, a man named Taylor Beedle, had never before visited Holliman, although it was known he had a large following in the city. Beedle, who held public office in a small Southern town, was out to widen his reputation; thus, the current concert. He had won each of his elections to the state assembly by razor-thin margins, a testament to the always fierce contention between those who hated him and those who thought his ideas had merit. Since Holliman had a considerable black population, the city began to divide into factions. There was a restlessness in the street that slowly turned to anger. Heavily armed police in fortified plastic masks, and holding back infuriated German shepherds, began to show up in great numbers to keep the peace. The Holliman police chief drove through the streets announcing, through a megaphone, that Holliman had always been the most crime-free little community in the Southern border area.

"We aim to keep it that way. Anyone who says no will find one of our little old puppies playing fast and loose with his throat."

During one rehearsal, the chief had paid a surprise visit to the theatre, arriving just as Han Nihsu was restaging the "Mad Dog Shooting" ballet number. Chorus kids, playing the parts of dicks, had dropped to their knees, and with whelping, animal cries were pumping out ammo at human-type targets. Confused by what he saw, the chief ducked behind a pillar.

"What the fuck?" he said as he whipped out his Colt .45 and blasted off a couple of rounds at the surprised chorus dicks.

Fortunately, the bullets were wide of the mark. Quickly realizing his mistake, the law officer got to his feet and sheepishly apologized to Han Nihsu for his quick trigger. He then explained the local situation and advised the members of the cast to stay huddled in their hotel rooms at night and not venture out into the street.

"That's when the trouble-mongers will make their move. We'll be there to give them a warm welcome."

Han Nihsu, with courage enough for the whole company, had not quite forgiven the chief for interrupting her dance rehearsal, and lashed out at him.

"I'd heard that Holliman was a wonderful place and told these kids they'd love it—and then you had to come in here and fart up the works."

The chief said he was sorry once again, and really seemed ashamed of himself. Half an hour after he'd left, a Holliman police sergeant arrived on the set with a small van carrying cheeseburgers and chocolate shakes for the entire cast. A note accompanied the food.

> "To a dear little lady who sure is full of beans and who I hope will be my guest one of these days for a little private soiree when the heat around here dies down."
>
> Bill Moaney
> Chief of Police, Holliman

"Horny bastard," said Han Nihsu, digging into a burger. "That'll be the day."

Gurney ate one of the free cheeseburgers, too, even though they were designated for the cast only. He wondered how all the strife and turmoil in the streets, and the presence of the hate-mongering Taylor Beedle, would affect the opening of *Violencia.*

My God, he thought, *hasn't this production had trouble enough already?*

All night long, Gurney listened to the unrelenting whine of police sirens as squad cars crammed with dicks and dogs roamed the streets, breaking up fights between hate-spewing Beedle followers (Beedle-ettes, they were called) and blacks, who were joined by a surprise contingent of rugged Lubavitchers bused in for the occasion. At one point, a *Violencia* dog broke loose and fought one of the Holliman shepherds to a bloody draw before the fight could be stopped. Several cops, who had observed the brawl, conceded that the showbiz hound had more than held his own and might have come out on top had the fight been permitted to go the distance.

As for Gurney, he felt that he could certainly take care of himself in the streets, but there was no point in looking for trouble, particularly with *Violencia* about to open. So he stationed himself on his lovely terrace; from there, he could see not only the Holliman Theatre, all gaily bedecked with signs announcing the premiere of what he thought of as "my show," but also the auditorium where Taylor Beedle's "Hate Concert" was to get under way that very same night.

Immediately before the opening, Philip Undertag appeared at the theatre with Beedle himself, plus a cortege of security guards. He had evidently brought the demagogue over in a spirit of good public relations.

After the producer had introduced various members of the staff, he gestured toward Gurney and said: "This is our writer."

"My aim," said Beedle, ignoring this information and directing his remarks to Undertag, "is to have the colored and the Jew—since that is what you appear to be, sir—live in peace and harmony, and the rest of us live in peace and harmony, too, only somewhere else. I am often misunderstood on this point."

Gurney was somewhat flustered by the appearance of the demagogue, perhaps because he knew he was supposed to hate him and didn't quite know how to express this sentiment.

"You're not as tall as I thought you'd be," he said to Beedle. "Then again, you're not so small, either. Additionally, you're not as fat or as thin as I thought you'd be."

"What do you mean?" said Beedle.

"Just what I said," Gurney said, bluffing his way along and pretending to be more enigmatic than he really was.

Undertag put his arm around the up-and-coming hate-monger.

"Tayler here is putting on a little show down the road. I hope it doesn't turn out to be a turkey like one of mine."

"He's had turkeys galore," said Gurney, joining in on the fun. "You might say he's been running a little turkey farm for himself."

Undertag threw Gurney a fierce look, indicating that he did not like to be teased about his flops—unless he was the one who did the teasing. Still, Gurney enjoyed Undertag's sly and waspish way of handling the demagogue.

One of Beedle's guards stepped forward smartly and presented Undertag with a placard:

"Happiness is having *Violencia* one street down from our Hate Concert, both shows competing in law and harmony for the ticket buyer's dollar and the two shows doing a whale of a business, since there is probably room for both."

Undertag was caught off guard by what appeared to be a gift of some kind and reacted by signaling to his PR person, Nettie Hersel. Thinking quickly this time, Nettie excused herself and rounded up a pair of Hobie Hancock's old ballet tights. After putting a decorative ribbon around them, she presented the garment to Tayler Beedle.

"These belong to our costar."

It was her idea, or so it appeared to Gurney, that one of Beedle's higher-ups, or even the demagogue himself, might be secretly turned on by the flimsy garment.

Beedle didn't seem to know what to make of the offering. But with a typical politician's reluctance to offend, he slipped Hancock's tights into his pocket and thanked both Nettie and Undertag for the thought.

Four days of getting accustomed to the new theatre flashed by. *Violencia* opened once again to a packed house, this time made up almost exclusively of Holliman people who were on a subscription list and were known to be interested, if not avid, theatregoers. As a result of the commotion caused by Taylor Beedle's nearby Hate Concert, an armed cortege of Holliman police formed a human funnel through which the opening-night playgoers were squired safely into the theatre. Gurney felt a little funny about not having Angela there for the opening, but she had been thoughtful enough to send a telegram, which made him feel a lot better. Surprisingly, his ex-wife sent one along, too. He was happy to have it, but it also made him feel slightly uncomfortable, since he had such mixed feelings about her.

Just before the overture, Gurney was handed yet another congratulatory telegram, from, of all people, his mother. This astonished him, since Babs Gurney had been dead for six years and could not possibly have gotten off the message to him. As he read it through, the literary style tipped him off that his ex-wife had sent this one, too, signing it with his mother's name. There was no question in Gurney's mind that she had guessed the message would lift his spirits, but it struck him as being a curious and somewhat tasteless thing to do, however well-motivated. As the curtain went up, he thought of his beloved mother, and it was all he could do to keep from crying. After pulling himself together, he promised to let Gilda Gurney know that she was never to do this again, since her gesture obviously had the reverse effect from its intended one.

It was clear from the start that *Violencia* would come off a lot more appealingly in Holliman than it had in Winslow. The cast, rested and chipper, performed with verve and confidence. And the stage crew, comfortable now with Bess Filimino's delicate sets, swung them in and out of the wings with the required casualness. The scenes themselves moved briskly along, one blending seamlessly into another. Norman Welles' upbeat new tunes were greeted with some enthusiasm. It helped, too, that cocker spaniel puppies were being used on stage in place of the snarling, chained-up rottweilers that had so unsettled the opening-night audience in Winslow, particularly the first dozen or so rows. All of the growl and sourness and abrasion had gone out of the show, but the Holliman theatregoers seemed held by it all the same. By the time the curtain came down on Act One, only half a dozen people at most had left their seats, several of them to use the rest rooms.

At the intermission, many of the playgoers passed up the chance to refresh themselves with lemonades and rushed over to get a look at the goings-on outside the Hate Concert auditorium. Most of the cast dashed over, too, several of them narrowly averting being smashed over the head with truncheons by police who mistakenly took them to be street rowdies. The two opposing factions faced off across the tense police lines, Beedle-ettes and their supporters on one side, the black citizens and Lubavitchers on the other, snarling and spitting at each other. Safe inside the auditorium, heavily protected by security guards, Taylor Beedle, using a bullhorn, egged on the crowd with his smoothly incendiary message; the sense of it was that although it was primarily blacks and Jews who were behaving poorly, there were others, such as Italians, who were causing trouble as well.

"You know who you are," he said menacingly, "and if you don't, we will come to your hallowed house and remind you."

Gurney was annoyed with the cast for standing around and watching the grim spectacle. Surely they were not there to pick up acting tips. And he certainly hoped they would be able to get back to the theatre in time for the start of Act Two. With all its potential for mass citywide slaughter, the Hate Concert scene had a kind of malevolent sweep to it that made Gurney long for the original version of *Violencia*. Whatever its flaws, he had a feeling it would have been proudly able to match Taylor Beedle's Hate Concert, moment for murderous moment. As it was, you could hardly blame the audience for leaving the new folksy, only mildly violent musical for a taste of the real thing.

And leave they did, all through the second act, clusters of them slipping off to the Hate Concert for fast peeks. But perhaps to the credit of the new, brisk, and fast-paced peppy little family musical, they all came back to the theatre and were on hand to give the cast three curtain calls—two of them unmistakably sincere. (A third was somewhat forced on them by the assistant stage manager, who raised the curtain as the audience, obviously sick of applauding, was filing out of the theatre.)

Hartog stood anonymously in the back of the theatre so that no one would hound him for his autograph. His summary of the performance was enigmatic.

"I'm not saying we ever had 'em," he said to Gurney, "but at least we didn't lose 'em."

Undertag and Toileau, who had flown in for the Holliman opening, were on hand, checking reactions in the rear of the theatre.

Generally a fashion plate, Toileau was wearing a fedora with a feather in it and a suit that was several sizes too small. Gurney guessed that the outfit was a deferential homage to the people of small-town Holliman.

"Special thanks to you, Paul," said Toileau, "for your gracious 'doody' cut.

"I think we would have lost 'em," he added, turning to Hartog, "if we had kept it in."

"I don't," said Hartog, stiffly. "But you might be right. I just don't know anymore.

"Does anyone?" he asked aggressively, thrusting his chin in Toileau's face.

"If we come in a hit," said Undertag cheerfully, "I'm buying everyone an interest in a hockey team."

Gurney was caught up in the general enthusiasm and only half-listening. In spite of himself, he felt a current of excitement flash across his shoulders. He had no idea why excitement always hit him in the shoulders.

Gurney pictured himself with brooding, knitted eyebrows, sitting grandly in important East Coast theatrical hangouts, wearing a cloak, casually tossing off interviews, his dialogue shot through with enigma, and being hailed as the season's most fascinating playwright. He was particularly pleased when several theatregoers, who recognized him from the program, asked him for his autograph.

"I'll take one, too, if you don't mind," said a jowly young chap, pushing his way past the others. Gurney saw that it was Norbert Tiomkins, his old classmate who had been so bitterly offended in Winslow.

"And I mean that about the autograph, Paul," said Tiomkins. "I followed you all the way to Holliman and I just want to say that you've pulled off the impossible. Hats off to you, Paul, and I hope you can find it in your heart to forgive that remark I made."

"Which one was that?"

"About not wanting to shit on the best part of you and your wife. It was said in the heat of anger."

"Oh well, in that case. . . ," said Gurney, with a gracious wave.

Backstage, there was tremendous exhilaration, with several of the male chorus fellows whom Gurney had assumed were gay saying they were so convinced *Violencia* was a hit that they had gone ahead and told their wives to order complete dinette sets for their apartments.

Gurney felt proud of his contribution to the show at this point, and also a heavy responsibility to continue making improvements until its success was assured. A pair of older female singers, cast in the roles of tough desk sergeants, grabbed Gurney and took turns forcing their tongues down his throat, stopping to say "Brilliant" and then continuing on with even deeper thrusts. The young delicious chorus kids, including Holly, his favorite, yanked at Clement Hartog's clothes. In a totally shameless manner they stroked his pelvis as they squealed happily and thanked him for directing them to theatrical glory. Gurney was a bit annoyed and jealous. He would not have minded having *his* pelvis stroked as well. But then he decided that his collaborator was entitled to a special treat. Especially since Essie had always kept such a strict eye on him and seen to it that he hadn't run off and slept with anyone.

The high spirits continued right along to the Broadway Grotto, a traditional hangout for traveling show folk, where Undertag had arranged to throw a victory party for the cast. When the celebration was under way, Holly took Gurney aside momentarily. Her body was soaked, as if she had been dipped in oil.

"What about those great times you were going to show me in Holliman, Mr. Scribe?"

Before Gurney could respond, one of Han Nihsu's assistants yanked her away, after giving the ex-homicider a wide-toothed grin. Gurney could not understand what she saw in the fellow. His guess was she liked him because he knew exactly how to handle her tricky little body and had quite a bit of trickiness of his own to match hers.

Gurney got drunk that night, on both high spirits and good Scotch. But he could remember only going to bed alone, after being confident he would somehow end up with one of the hot young chorus kids or, at the very minimum, with a tongue-thrusting older female singer. He had a momentary pang of loneliness, feeling foolish about having four beds in the suite and only himself to fill them. But ultimately it was tolerable. He also had the glad, secure feeling that *Violencia,* for all of its woes, was going to be a smash after all.

Scene 12

The next morning, he was awakened by a call from his ex-wife.

"How do you *feel*? I mean, God, you must be sick to your stomach, you poor thing."

"What do you mean?" asked Gurney, still not sure whether he was in Winslow or Holliman or at Angela's apartment.

"Oh, my God, that's right," she said. "I just realized that you don't know. Not if you just got up. I should have known that would happen. Oh well, so long as I woke you up, I might as well tell you that the reviews are awful. They're so bad that frankly I feel a little funny about saying who I was once married to. I can't help it, Paul. I've got to be honest. You know that was the one thing you could always count on with me."

Gurney wondered why she would have gone to all that trouble to get the Holliman papers—not an easy assignment on the East Coast—but then he chalked it up to simple curiosity. *Oh well,* he thought, *at least I've gotten the bad news short and sweet and don't have to have the whole process dragged out.*

"Look, go back to bed and try to get some sleep," she said, "and I'm sorry I got you up. I probably never should have made this call."

Gurney allowed himself a moment of self-pity.

"You won't have to worry about an opening-night gown now, Gilda."

"No," she said. "Some other time. But listen, would you have taken me?"

"I don't think so."

"Then fuck you, buster," she said, and hung up.

Behind the anger, Gurney realized, there had been plenty of hurt as well. He ordered a giant breakfast, considering himself quite brave for doing so. When it arrived, he took one bite of his omelette and pushed it aside. Dipping into the morning paper, he read a bit of the review, but found he couldn't take much of that, either.

SHOULD HAVE KEPT IT THE WAY
IT WAS IN WINSLOW

"Several years ago, this critic sat through an infuriatingly witless little trifle called *Hats Ahoy,* which he promptly labeled the single worst load of tripe ever to be slung together in the history of the modern theatre as we know it. Well, all I can say is, move over, *Hats Ahoy.* Triumphant new recipient of the World's Worst Dog is the aptly titled *Violencia,* a musical which creaked open last night at the Holliman and did such *violence* to the eyes, ears, nose, and overall sanity of this reviewer, it just about drove him out of his beloved business."

Gurney laid the the paper aside and received a call from Undertag.

"How were the others?" he asked the producer.

"Let's just say that the one you read was a rave. You'd better come up to my suite."

*   *   *

"I'm out of the business, fellas," said Norman Welles, pacing up and down in front of the three producers and Clement Hartog. "This just about does it for me. Name one person who'll work with me after this. I've never gotten notices like that in my life and all I can say is it's a lucky thing I've got a few bucks put away. I'm just going to scoop up Tippy, whom I'm pleased to say I'm in love with again, and go off to Mexico for a while. Both of us will lie around, enjoy the quiet down there, and figure out what my next move is—or whether I even *have* a next move."

"Norman has graciously consented to let us use his songs," said Undertag, "even though he personally is getting out."

"We're very disturbed," said Toileau. " I thought taking out 'doody' would do a lot more for us than it did."

"I thought you fellows liked the show," said Hartog with great calm.

The director had evidently decided to make a fight of it. His remark caught the producing team off guard.

"We did," said Undertag.

"Then what changed your mind?"

"We slept on it and sort of thought it over," said Undertag.

"I don't believe that," said Hartog. "I think you've been rattled by the notices. I have been too, frankly, but I'm still in the ball game. And may I remind you, gentlemen, that you are sitting in a hotel in Holliman and that the good gray *New York Times* hasn't said a word about *Violencia*."

"You've got to admit, Clement," said Toileau, "that we're losing 'em."

"Assuming we ever had 'em," said Undertag in a sly, stand-up-comedian style.

"*Who*, exactly, are we losing?" said Hartog, showing his teeth.

Whether it was for the love of *Violencia* or to save his mom's career, Gurney didn't particularly care.

"Clement's right," said Gurney. "In Winslow, we drove close to two thousand people out of the theatre. Last night, in Holliman, we didn't drive anyone out."

"Keeping them in is one thing," Mandarin interjected. "Making them happy is another."

Gurney was aware there was considerable friction between Hartog and Mandarin.

"How do you know they weren't happy?" said Hartog, raising his voice this time. He had more than an inkling that Mandarin was after his job, and he was probably dead right. "Did you sit down and ask them? How the fuck do you know, you little fart?"

"I'm no little fart," said Mandarin. "Say what you will, but that is not a fair and accurate description of me."

"All right, all right," said Undertag, patting the air with his palms in a peacemaking gesture. Gurney was beginning to see that the man could not bear confrontation. "Clement, you'd probably never speak to me again if I locked up the show right now, is that right? And you'd probably bad-mouth me on both coasts, am I correct? Tell everyone that I deserve my turkeys?"

"Knock it off, Philip," said Hartog. "I don't feel well."

"Tell you what," said the producer. "We'll give you a week. You boys deserve a chance to pull this show off. Toileau and I will fly back to Holliman next weekend. If we like what we see, we'll bring it in. If not, we bury the body."

"I still don't get it," said Hartog. "You *loved* the show before the notices came in."

"We did love it," said Toileau. "But we decided we didn't love it as much as we thought we did. It sort of fooled us."

Norman Welles shot out of Holliman like a thief in the night, without even saying good-bye.

"Cocksucker," said Hartog.

"Motherfucker," said Gurney.

The two sere sitting around in Gurney's suite.

"He certainly does take care of his own ass," said the director. "Well, maybe he knows something that we don't."

"Oh hell, Clement," said Gurney, "the poor bastard's got nothing left in the tank."

"He had nothing much to start with," said Hartog. "Why, oh why, did I ever get involved with that asshole? And I let him get away with those ridiculous French love songs, too. In a show about *homicide*. I may have to see a shrink about this."

"We're both at fault, Clement."

"I think we can turn it around," said Hartog. "I still believe in this goddamned show. There's just too much that's good there for us not to fight for it down to the wire. And don't forget, Paul, that if the show dies in Holliman, your column, 'Ask Gurney,' and those wonderful issues of *The Homicider* will never see the light of day on the stage as long as you live."

Gurney thought Hartog's argument in this case was ill-chosen, one of the few times the director was wildly off target. Perhaps it was presumptuous, but Gurney felt that no matter what the theatrical fate of *Violencia,* nothing could tarnish his popular advice column and his achievements at the helm of the monthly *Homicider. What if some film company made a farcical and preposterous movie of* Anna Karenina? *he asked himself. Would it tarnish the great Russian classic one bit? Not on your life.* So Hartog's argument that a theatrical bomb could alter the standing of his "Ask Gurney" column and of his magazines (which he'd had bound in leather, incidentally) was no way to reach Gurney.

He had been shaken by the rough notices himself, but he had no intention of pulling a Norman Welles and checking out. For one thing, he had no place in particular to go, no one to go back to but Angela—and he could always bring her to Holliman. And there might still be some fun to be had in sticking around. Holly, for example, seemed to be tiring of the four Balinese assistant choreographers and was probably about ready to drop into his lap.

And, of course, the main reason he couldn't bring himself to leave was that he had no heart to desert Clement Hartog.

"I honestly feel we can pull it off," said Hartog, with a plea in his eyes. "Don't you, Paul?"

"Yes, I do."

"Then how?" said the director. "Tell me how on God's earth we can do it. And then I'll know."

Clement Hartog got a bad case of the shakes then. He hugged himself and began to cry.

Gurney thought it best to walk out to the terrace and look down on the suddenly quiet streets of Holliman—and pretend he hadn't seen any of this.

Hartog's loss of confidence was only temporary, however. Shaky, but determined, the two collaborators rolled up their sleeves and tore into the show once again. Treating *Violencia* as if it were a seriously ill patient instructed to go on a crash diet, Hartog suggested they cut away everything—everything—that displeased them in the slightest way. That meant most of the songs and almost all of the second act. The team nevertheless proceeded with the surgery, feeling giddy as they slashed away at all of the doubtful material. But when they were finished they realized they were down to three songs in the entire show—and a six-minute second act.

When the cast performed the show in its new whittled-down condition, Holliman playgoers began to boo and then to file out in droves, feeling they'd been had.

"I didn't pay good money to see a sketch," said one disgruntled subscriber.

"That's all right," said Hartog. "I'm not worried about them. This is Holliman, and our target is New York. I'll admit we don't have much, but what we've got is gold, and we can always build from it."

But building from gold meant the insertion of new songs, and the team suddenly realized they didn't have a composer. Certainly neither Gurney nor Hartog was about to start writing music. Most of the established composers were at work on shows of their own, but there was one—a certain Hilton Numero—who was reported to be at large, having had a show of his own turn out to be a disaster. Yet Hartog was somewhat reluctant to contact the talented music man.

"He once called me down to Philadelphia for an opinion on a show he was doing that was struggling. I hated it and didn't even pay him the courtesy of going backstage to see him and tell him my feelings. But I'm not denying that it would be great if we could get him."

Hartog decided to swallow his pride and call Numero.

"So this is Hartog, is it? " said Numero. "I've been waiting for this call for a long, long time. Will I do your show? Of course I won't, you no-talent, ill-mannered slob fuck. Nyah, nyah, nyah," he shouted into the receiver, and then hung up.

"Figures," said Hartog, not in the least surprised.

Mandarin finally pitched in and came up with a two-woman composer-lyricist team that was responsible for many new rock favorites and reportedly capable of delivering an entirely fresh score in two days. Talking to them over drinks, Gurney realized something awful about himself: He had reached the point where he really didn't care whether they came up with anything or not.

A piano was wheeled into the suite of the two women, who stayed up all night, during which time they wrote four new songs. Hartog, in an adjoining suite, had remained awake, crouching, his ear to the paper-thin walls. He called Gurney first thing in the morning.

"Don't even get out of bed, Paul. They're awful."

Evidently the two women, who had been highly critical of Welles' Paris compositions, had simply stepped up the tempo on them and shifted the settings to downtown Prague . . . so that now the romantic songs were about star-crossed lovers wandering along Czech viaducts.

"We were better off with Paris," said Hartog.

One afternoon, Mandarin paid a visit to Gurney in his hotel suite. The associate producer, whose bruised face was covered with adhesive tape, said he had been mistaken for a male hustler and had been beaten up pretty badly by local welders.

"I'm sorry, Mandarin," said Gurney.

"Can't take an innocent midnight stroll along the waterfront and even *glance* at someone," said Mandarin. "But forget that. I'll just stop being so trusting from now on. Now look, I've been trying to help you guys, am I right? I brought down the two girls. I appealed to Numero to forgive and forget. Was it my fault that neither deal worked out?"

"Not to my knowledge," said Gurney.

"And I'm still going to keep at it," said Mandarin, "because, don't kid yourself, if you guys go down the tubes, I stand to take a financial bath myself. But look, life goes on—would you disagree with that?"

"No, I wouldn't."

"I'm glad, because that's why I'm here."

He then proposed that Gurney work with him on a new show he had planned, a rock version of the Job story, to be set in a once-restricted country club on the outskirts of Ottawa that now admitted just about anybody. Gurney thought the idea had merit—

especially since shows with rock scores had been doing well on Broadway.

"I'd be happy to kick it around once we wrap up *Violencia.*"

"I'm talking about right now."

"Now?" said Gurney. "You want me to work on it now, while the goddamned ship is sinking? What kind of third-rate rat do you think I am?"

"What would you be doing right this second?" asked Mandarin. "I mean if I wasn't here?"

"Oh, just sitting around, I guess, relaxing, waiting for Clement to get here so we can start thinking of ways to save *Violencia.*

"That's my point," said Mandarin. "That's the time I'm talking about. When you're sitting around, relaxing. Talking about *Hey, Job!* will *help* you to relax like you've never relaxed in your life. It will take you out of *Violencia,* and you'll return to it with a fresh perspective."

"I'd feel like a swine," said Gurney. "If Clement ever found out, I'd never be able to face him."

"Don't kid yourself. With all due respect, he's probably working on three backup shows himself, in case this one tanks."

"Clement wouldn't do that. Not Clement."

"How much time do we have now?" asked Mandarin.

"He'll be down in half an hour."

"Shall we try to get in a quick session?"

"Oh, what the hell."

The awful truth was that Gurney, deep in his soul, and even not so deep, had lost all heart to go on with *Violencia.* Just as he felt he had let the show down, he felt that *Violencia* had let him down as well. He had liked the craggy sourness of it in Winslow and the fact that it might make some money. But in its current stripped-down, antiseptic condition, he wasn't terribly proud of it. He knew that he

was just hanging around for a little showbiz action, as if he were
trying to fondle an accident victim.

Though he had come down hard on Norman Welles, it could
be argued, he knew, that the composer had been the honest one on
the team. Crawling with guilt, Gurney now met the slippery and
ambitious Mandarin for clandestine sessions on *Hey, Job!*—which,
quite frankly, he enjoyed more than the work with Hartog on
Violencia. At least it was fresh. He now saw *Violencia* as a great,
spoiled cheese, with pieces flaking off, one by one. Meeting Mandarin
was like having a rendezvous with a secret lover.

I guess I'm just a promiscuous person, he told himself.

With Mandarin at his side, he would sit at his desk, taking
notes and keeping an ear cocked for the sound of Hartog's weary
footsteps. When he heard the director approach, he would fling the
Hey, Job! script into a drawer, slam it shut, then leap onto the couch,
cross his legs, and treacherously pretend that he and Mandarin were
racking their brains, trying to think of composers who might help
out on poor *Violencia*.

Only once did Gurney come close to reversing his feelings
about the show. All along he had expressed the same sentiment to
Hartog (who, incidentally, sensed his disillusionment):

"Clement, do you realize that not one mature adult who has
seen the show and has some connection with the theatre has paid us
a compliment? If I could just hear one good thing from someone I
can respect—outside of our own group—perhaps I'd be encouraged."

One night, after slipping away from a secret session on *Hey,
Job!* Gurney joined the Hartogs for a preshow dinner at the Broadway Grotto. As he approached their table, Gurney realized there was
an individual present he did not recognize, someone who seemed
alien to the group but was evidently there to join them for dinner all
the same. Gurney's time at the Bureau had enabled him to recognize people from just a single feature—and he was confident he had
never met this man before. The fellow had pointed elf's ears and an

odd-shaped head. It was as if a spell had been cast on the Broadway Grotto—perhaps by this individual—and everyone within was caught in it. The man's face was unnaturally ruddy; he might have lived in some other world—perhaps in a forest among trolls. His eyes burned through little slits.

"Repeat to him what you just told us, Everett," said Hartog as Gurney pulled up a chair.

When the man spoke, it was with a lisp of a variety that Gurney had never before heard.

"I was just telling your friends that I think *Violencia* is a classic. It is my intention to communicate this feeling to Philip Undertag and tell him that he is a king-sized horse's ass if he even dreams about closing this gem here in Holliman."

The curious little fellow's size and appearance were misleading. Evidently, he was a man who spoke his mind in no uncertain terms. Gurney made no bones about the fact that he was thrilled. He was close to tears. The man turned out to be Everett Dondilee, an actors' agent who made it a point to attend out-of-town openings. He did this out of curiosity and also because he simply liked to keep posted on what was going on in the theatre. No one had invited him to see *Violencia* in far-off Holliman; he had simply come of his own accord. If he hadn't liked the show, he would quietly have gone back east and never said a word to anyone.

Gurney thought that if *Violencia* were indeed to become a smash, and the behind-the-scenes story to surface, one certainly would be able to point to a turning point in the show's fortunes: the sudden, unannounced appearance of this curious and delightful little man.

"When I look up on that stage," said Dondilee, "and I see Essie on her stilts, having highly charged verbal duels with her misbehaving detective son, I see my own dad and my own childhood. In my opinion, it's the story of every thinking American. My friends, it *is* the American story."

Dondilee gripped Gurney's arm. He had a bonfire in his eyes.

"Don't change a word of it, Gurns. And don't you dare let them close it on you."

"I won't, sir," said Gurney, who felt the strength pouring back into him and didn't even mind that he'd been addressed by that hateful nickname.

"And I want you to know," said Dondilee, looking away for the first time, "that all this has absolutely nothing to with the fact that my agency represents Essie Hartog. Not to speak of her son Clement, Matt Tanker, Hobie Hancock, and Han Nihsu, along with the four assistants. I'm this close to signing Ty Sabatini, but he hates to pay commissions."

When Gurney discovered that Dondilee represented virtually the entire cast, the last bit of confidence passed right out of him. It may very well have been that the agent had expressed his honest opinion of the show, but his could hardly have been considered an objective view. If *Violencia* were miraculously to come in as a hit, he stood to make a tidy sum on commissions. If the show closed in Holliman, he would not earn a quarter. Gurney desperately needed a shot in the arm, but not from the almost certainly biased Everett Dondilee. As soon as he realized the agent's motive, Gurney, with not a word to anyone, quietly gave up all hope for *Violencia*. He spent more time than ever with Mandarin on the promising *Hey, Job,* and merely went through the motions of collaborating with Hartog. And he wondered all the while what it was that kept him from throwing up his hands and leaving town.

Over the weekend, the inevitable came to pass. Toileau and Undertag, as promised, flew down, saw the revised show, then summoned Gurney and Hartog to a backstage meeting. It was held in the tiniest office Gurney had ever seen, Undertag having to sit on Toileau's lap so that all the principals could fit in.

"You boys have done some wonderful work," said Toileau, "but frankly, we're a little displeased."

"Oh?" said Hartog, feigning surprise. "How come?"

"Oh, cut it out, Clement," said Undertag. "You've only got two songs left in the show and your second act's four minutes long. I'm not bringing a ten-minute million-dollar skit to Broadway. If what I saw isn't a turkey, I'd like to know what is."

"What we've got is pure gold," said Hartog. "I've even thought of dropping those last two songs."

His face was drawn and his Adam's apple stuck out a country mile. It occurred to Gurney that he now knew exactly how Hartog would look in his coffin.

"Let's be frank, fellas," said Undertag, with a certain kindness in his voice. "Let's be men and do what we have to do."

Hartog tried to speak but could not find his voice. He looked over to Gurney for help. The librettist was aware that some determination on his part might very well turn the tide and convince the shaky producers that they ought to continue battling for the show. But he could not find the strength or ambition to carry the ball.

"I've always sort of liked the show," he said feebly.

"Sure, fella," said Undertag, patting his knee. "We'll post the closing notice tomorrow night. That will give you a chance to inform the kids, Clement."

Gurney had the feeling that the producer would excel at making consoling remarks to bereaved people at funerals.

The four men shook hands all around, over and over, as though they were afraid to stop.

"It's a funny thing," said Undertag, stopping for a moment before he squeezed his way out of the tiny office. "With all of my flops, I've never before closed one of them out of town. I've always given them a chance to be turkeys on Broadway."

Scene 13

Gurney knew that one thing he could not do was face the cast after the closing notice went up. He had always felt himself to be a bit of a hero to them, putting words in their mouths as he did, shaping and reshaping their characters and personalities. How would Holly look at him now, for example? As a fellow whose libretto had buried *Violencia*? As someone whose first try at a Broadway musical was so bad the show couldn't even make it to New York? Of course, he hadn't done too well with her before the closing notice, either. You never knew. Maybe she loved losers.

After the sad meeting with the producers, Gurney returned to his suite and started to pack a few things. Hartog walked in after him and rubbed his dried and aging hands.

"All right, let's go," he said.

"Where's that?" said Gurney.

"To work. This is a good time for it."

"I don't understand. The closing notice is up. What are we going to work on?"

"The show," said Hartog. "You don't think I'm going to quit, do you?"

"What's the point if it's all over? How the hell am I supposed to do anything when there's no chance the show will open?"

"Well, we're down here, aren't we? There's always a chance. Anything can happen. Fuck Undertag. I don't need him. I'll get another producer. I am bringing the motherfucker in, that's all. I'll beg and I'll steal and I'll plead and I'll bleed, but I am bringing this goddamned show in."

"Maybe I'd feel that way, too, if my mother were playing the lead," said Gurney.

And, of course, once he'd made the cruel remark he felt like cutting out his tongue.

Hartog took a long time before he replied.

"I knew you felt that way, Paul," he said, before opening the door to leave. "I just wish you hadn't said it."

Gurney waited around a few hours and then tried calling the director.

"I'm sorry," said the operator, "but Mr. Hartog is not taking any calls."

Gurney packed the rest of his things and started to walk out of the suite. Then he turned back and unpacked and spent the night in Holliman, not seeing anyone, not tellling anyone he was there. He decided there would be plenty of time to pull out the next morning.

After he'd ordered breakfast, Gurney realized it was his birthday. It had been years since this was a cause for any kind of celebration. But he was forty now. He had been led to believe he would now have a clear vision of the highway ahead, a knowledge of which dreams were possible, which were absurd. As he ate his French toast, he realized that his vision, sad to say, was still indistinct. His hope was that it would clear up as the day went along.

As Gurney finished his second cup of coffee, he remembered suggesting to Angela that they take an apartment together. She loved the idea and had immediately sublet her flat to a team of bachelor Armed Robbery detectives, and moved in with a girlfriend. As a result, Gurney, at least for the moment, had no place to stay in New York. He hung around the hotel a bit longer and did some drinking, and soon it was early evening. Hartog would be telling the cast about the closing notice about this time, he realized. In a sense, this represented an official good-bye to Gurney's adopted showbiz family. Prompted by that thought, he put in a call to his ex-wife at the home they'd shared on Staten Island—thinking perhaps he could spend a night or two with her to tide him over.

The phone was picked up by a man who sounded suspiciously like Detective Furbisher, an auto-thefter from his precinct.

"Wait a second, Paul," said the man, "and I'll let you talk to your old wife."

Moments later, Gilda Gurney picked up the phone.

"Why are you calling me?" she asked.

As she spoke, Gurney heard a chorus of hearty male voices in the background. It sounded like the late shift in the detectives' bullpen.

"They posted the closing notice tonight," said Gurney. "I'd like to come back and stay with you a while. Nothing serious. I have nowhere to go, and I don't think I can deal with a hotel."

"Oh, Paul, I'm sorry," she said. "I'm having a few of your old friends over for the weekend. Maybe we can meet for lunch sometime."

"Its my goddamned birthday, Gilda."

"I'm aware of that. I sent you an ashtray."

"I gave up smoking."

"And I'm supposed to know everything?"

Gurney hung up and realized, amazingly, that he had begun to cry. It was a most unusual experience, the first time he had ever broken into tears and not given himself plenty of advance warning; the first time that he hadn't been in on the planning of it. He was embarrassed by the tears, thinking of his old friends at the Bureau and how they would needle him if they ever discovered that he had let himself go in such a shameless manner. But you never knew—maybe they did a little secret crying, too. Maybe that could have been a number for *Violencia.*

> *Boo hoo*
> *Boo Hoo*
> *Tough detectives*
> *They cry, too.*

Maybe it would have saved the show.

She would *do that,* he thought. *She has some sense of timing. The night my show closes and she's rolling around on the carpet with all my old friends.* He realized, of course, that he had no right to feel that way and that it was her life to lead. There was also a possibility that she *wasn't* rolling around on the carpet. But this did not stop the tears. The liquor was partially responsible, and the crying probably had something to do with saying good-bye to the show as well. It was possible he loved *Violencia* more than he had realized. Was it his fault that he wanted it to be a hit all by itself; without any help from him?

When a room service man appeared with the club sandwich he had ordered, Gurney, still crying, asked the fellow if he'd like to have a drink.

"Take as much as you want," he said. "Empty the bottle. Take anything you see—my clothes, my money; none of it means anything to me."

"Maybe I will have a little nip," said the man.

And he did take a surprisingly modest one, considering the grandiose nature of the invitation.

"I guess you went and caught yourself a little cold," said the fellow.

It would have been impossible for him not to notice that Gurney was falling apart. Gurney was touched by his discretion.

"I been divorced," said the room service man. "Best thing
to do is move to another city. Interstate is the only way to handle
the bitch. You send her a check and chances are she won't cross
state lines."

The man had an uncanny way of getting right to the heart
of Gurney's difficulties. After he'd left, Gurney kept wondering
whether the man had known the librettist was crying or whether he'd
genuinely thought he had a cold or a mild flu attack. He continued
to ponder this question, which was obviously related to the larger
one of whether room service people could divine such things. Specu-
lating on the matter somehow lifted his spirits, and he soon felt surprisingly chipper. Since he had no place in particular to go, he decided
to attend the traditional "closing notice" party and to face the cast.
The appearance would make him seem like a hero; no one had to
know that the real reason he had remained behind was that his ex-
wife was taking on the entire Homicide Bureau.

As Gurney was trying to decide which of his two windbreak-
ers to wear, a call came through from a fellow who said he worked
for an East Coast newspaper. He had heard that the show had given
up the ghost.

"What our readers would like to know, sir, is how does it
feel to have one of these things shot down beneath your feet? What's
the sensation in your gut?"

"I haven't quite gathered my thoughts yet," said Gurney.

"Well, then, suppose I help you along. I'll give you some
choices and you tell me the one you'd like to put in: A—a sharp,
stabbing pain around the heart area; B—a dull sense of nausea in
the pit of the stomach; or C—a certain sense of nothingness, a
'What's-it-all-mean-anyway' attitude?"

"I'll have to get back to you," Gurney said, and hung up.

He stayed in the suite for another hour and then strolled into
the Broadway Grotto where the Hartogs and Han Nihsu were hav-

ing dinner. Clement Hartog was stunned to see Gurney. He jumped up and threw his arms around the ex-dick.

"Good Christ, Paul," said the enfeebled director, "you'll never know what this means to me."

Essie Hartog wept until lumps of her mascara began to drop into her minestrone soup. Han Nihsu hugged Gurney to her tight little body and rubbed her aging but tough little Asian buttocks back and forth across his thighs.

"I just couldn't see my way through to abandoning you folks," said Gurney, lying through his teeth.

"God will reward you for this," said Essie Hartog. "And you'll see: We're going to bring in a smash yet. I'll do everything in my power to get your precious lines exactly right. And I know they love me out there."

"Let's not talk about that, Mother," said Hartog, in one of the rare instances of his acknowledging their close tie. "What's important is that Paul stayed here after the closing notice was posted. He's going to be here and look the kids in the eyes. I want you to know, Paul, that they took it like thoroughbreds. You would have been proud of them."

The four talked about the good times they'd had in preparing the show. And then Essie went out to do her evening performance. Standing proudly on a pair of gift stilts from the cast, she turned in the acting job of her life. Watching the pared-down *Violencia,* Paul Gurney realized he was seeing his once-beloved baby for the last time in his life, even though the show, by contract, had a full week to run.

A great cry of excitement could be heard when Gurney walked into the closing night party. After an argument with Norman Welles, Tippy had flown back to Holliman to be with the cast in its last days. And she had graciously consented to have the party in her suite.

Holly was one of the first to approach Gurney.

"I thought you were going to disappear and not say good-bye," confided the wiry little dancer. "I said to myself, *I'll never forgive that guy if he does that.* How come you decided to stick around?"

"Leaving's easy," said Gurney, looking philosophically off in the distance. "Anyone can do that. It's the other that's tough."

As Holly pondered the thought, one of the female singers came over and once again, in what seemed to be a trademark greeting of hers, thrust her tongue deep into Gurney's throat.

"You're a major artist," she said. "And you are ahead of your time."

"I don't know," said Gurney, hoping she wasn't getting set to deal out another sensuous kiss. "Sometimes I think I didn't do a good enough job."

"It was *too* good. That's where you went wrong."

The party then took on a drugged and slightly out-of-focus quality. Restraints were abandoned, with people walking about in a tilted, slow-motion gait, as though they were on the deck of a sinking liner—which in a sense, of course, they were. The male chorus boys no longer bothered to disguise their sexual preferences. They put on elaborate jewelry, changed into skirts and peasant blouses, applied makeup liberally, and broke into dance numbers from shows that had been successful. The unmistakable odor of hashish was in the air. Gurney had some expertise in this area. He had been in on raids and watched junk dicks, after a drug seizure, sit around and smoke up samples to make sure it was the real thing.

With his eyes filmed over, Ty Sabatini lay back on a bed with two female singers, openly stroking them between their legs and meeting with only halfhearted opposition. Gurney thought he saw Clement Hartog applying a great blue-black gash of lipstick. He turned away, not wanting to know about that particular tendency of the director.

A jewelry-bedecked Hobie Hancock approached Gurney and gave him a wet earlobe kiss.

"C'est la vie, Monsieur Paul. Thanks for giving my dormant career a much-needed zetz."

Matt Tanker squatted on the floor as if he were sitting at a campfire. It was his feeling that Gurney's concept of the show had been a mistaken one.

"I believe it should have been all about me—my narration, my voice throughout, sort of my trip; Essie singing now and then, but me, in a sense, continually drowning her out. That's where you went astray. But I want you to know I don't resent in the least giving up a booming medical practice. At least I got to get into myself . . . in addition to sleeping with just about every girl in the show . . . Tippy, Holly, you know the list. . . . except Essie, of course, although, believe me, she was lined up and ready to go. . . . But don't be misled . . . it was just plain old-fashioned sex . . . stick it in, take it out. . . . I did not get into their heads."

Gurney was impressed by how quickly Tanker had gone from being a hotshot Beverly Hills chiropractor to a laid-back Marin County dropout. He didn't even resent the former sex patroller for sleeping with all the girls in the show, although he would have preferred that Holly hadn't made the cut. Still, Tanker's style was so vague and free-floating that the girls probably hadn't even noticed they'd slept with him.

Essie Hartog dragged Gurney into another room and thanked him again and again, allowing, perhaps unconsciously, one of her giant torpedoing bosoms to slip into his mouth. Gurney quite diplomatically rejected the mammary, pretending it had never been proffered. He looked for Holly, who was pinned inside a shower stall by two of the young Balinese assistant choreographers. Is that all they did, he wondered, just pin her to the walls inside shower stalls? Didn't they ever have higher thoughts?

For the first time, Gurney behaved like a real management fellow and elbowed them aside, dragging Holly's tricky little body outside to the hotel corridor.

"I never let them near me," she said. "It only looks that way. It's always been you, Mr. Gurney . . . Paul, if I may."

I'll bet, he thought. When he finally had the squirming little dancer alone in his suite, he took her out to his terrace, feeling that the lovely view would make a nice change from her own congested little quarters and possibly be exciting.

"Pop this under my nose," she said, handing him a gelatin capsule. "It'll send me through the roof."

Gurney followed her instructions, taking a fast sniff himself and then waving the crushed object beneath the dancer's nostrils. Fingers of blood pumped out of her nose in great jets; he never would have guessed they could have come from so fragile a girl. Somewhat panicked, he tried to stop the flow with a towel. What if this was *it* for her, and she never came to? The press would probably pick it up. And that's all he would need—*Chorus Cutie O.D.'s in Suite of Ex-Dick Librettist.*

At a loss as to what to do next, he slid the dancer under the bed and sat on it. When he saw that this was a poor solution, he slid her out again and carried her back to the party. He felt a little sheepish about this, holding her as if he was on his way to the post office to return a package that had been mistakenly delivered to him. By the time they got back to the party, the blood flow had stopped.

"Hi, fellas," she said brightly to a pair of Han Nihsu's assistants, putting her arms around their tightly muscled East Asian shoulders.

"Hi, pussy-pants," said one of them, as they scooped her up and took her into a bathroom.

Later, as he strolled by, Gurney saw them popping capsules freely beneath her nose while she giggled and slipped her mischievous tongue in and out of their eager little Balinese mouths.

Gurney saw all of this as a clear-cut demonstration that she was "chorus" and he was "management." They existed in separate worlds—his clean and wholesome, hers unbearably sexy—and he might as well wash his hands of her . . . unless he wanted to take dancing lessons and become a high-kicking, middle-aged chorus boy. There was also the stray possibility that she really didn't like him that much. Whatever the case, he made a vow that when he got back to the East Coast, he would not call her for dinner unless he had absolutely nothing else to do.

Much more important to him was that he had finally made it to one of the orgies—even if as a nonparticipant. As he sat in the center of the room, drugged and bleary-eyed, but somewhat happy, one of the chorus people, a fellow known for his hawklike temper, approached him.

"This," he said, "has got to be the dullest party we've had since the start of rehearsals."

Just as Gurney had suspected, the uninhibited bashes had been going on night after night without him. *Oh well,* he thought, *at least I got to attend one of them.* He felt that on a night like this it was almost against the law to end up alone. In that spirit, he looked around for Tippy and saw that she was in close colloquy with Matt Tanker. Evidently she had decided to spend a sexually laid back night with him.

Gurney returned to his suite, sharing the elevator with one of the great-breasted sopranos. As they stopped at his floor, he said, "Oh hell, come on along with me," and pulled her into his suite. He undressed her and sucked her great breasts in the moonlight, but decided after a few minutes that it was a hollow and pointless activity.

* * *

In the darkness of his suite, Gurney called Angela and told her the official notice had gone up and that perhaps the two of them ought to take a vacation on some island or other.

"I can't believe this," she said. "It's much too good a thing to happen."

The next morning Gurney went to Hartog's room and told the director he was really leaving this time. Hartog made a last feeble effort to keep him in Holliman.

"I'm bringing a major producer down to see the show. Kermit enjoys a good crapshoot and likes nothing better than to beat the odds. If he sees something in the show that he likes, he just might gamble and bring it in."

"I can't deal with it," said Gurney. "You're looking at a dead man."

Gurney was far from being a corpse when he said that. In many ways, he was spilling over with suppressed energy. What he meant was that he was frustrated and lonely. Had the rascally little Holly dashed in that moment and flown at his body, for example, his outlook would have changed immediately.

Hartog paused a moment, then set him free.

"I understand, Paul. And I know where you are. I've never been there myself, but I do understand. And I want you to know that I'll never forget what you did for the cast by staying an extra day. One more day would be even more useful, but I don't want to push you."

Gurney let the hint go by. He gave Hartog a quick hug and swept out of the room. After checking the lobby to make sure there were no cast members about—he'd had his fill of good-byes—Gurney slipped out of the hotel and took a slow, mournful drive back to New York. On the one hand, he felt awful about not staying to see the show interred once and for all. But at the same time, he found that he was light and easy behind the wheel, as though orders had arrived to remove a giant weight from his back. Before driving to his ex-wife's house, he stopped off at midnight to call Angela, and arranged to pick her up in his car. Once he had done so, he parked on a deserted street and wanted to make love to her then and there, but she turned him down.

"Not in the car," she said.

It was the first time she had ever rejected him, which seemed to be of importance, although he didn't know why. And out of nowhere, she said she needed to visit her parents, who were retired prison guards, on the Jersey shore.

After dropping off Angela at her folks' place, Gurney drove over to his ex-wife's small ranch house, wondering if he would discover her on a chandelier with one of his old Homicide buddies. He tried to imagine what he would do—sail into the fellow and pummel him to the ground with outraged blows? Or take the high road—simply turn around disdainfully as if he had no time for trivialities?

He could hardly wait to find out which course he would take.

As it happened, Gilda Gurney was alone. They sat together and had a few brandies. Amazingly, she had completed her decorating scheme for the house, something he had been after her to do for years. When they were together, her style had been to bring each room frustratingly close to completion and then to stop cold, leaving a third of the room bare and unfurnished. Only after he left had she been able to go the distance on decorating. Was that true of their love life as well? He left that door unopened.

Gurney stayed over that night, thinking for a moment that he might slip into bed with her for old times' sake and perhaps give her a few hugs and light squeezes. Who knows where it might lead—possibly to a fresh new marriage? But he held off and slept in the second bedroom, a bit tensely. In the morning he got a call from Mandarin, who had somehow tracked him down.

"How would you like to go to the Caribbean for a few weeks, all expenses paid, to rest up and do a little fiddling with *Hey, Job!*"

The call was a nice shot in the arm. It was good to know he was in demand. Gurney told Mandarin it sounded great, but that he would only go on one condition.

"What's that?" asked Mandarin.

"That my friend Angela gets to come, too."

"She the one with the great body?" asked Mandarin.

"That's her, all right. She's highly intelligent, too, and has a wonderful family background."

"Bring her along," said Mandarin. "She sounds like a good kid."

Gurney thought it over and decided it was an excellent idea to go away for a rest, even though he wasn't particularly tired. But there was no need to bring Mandarin into the picture. Added to which, he didn't particularly feel like working on *Hey, Job!* It would certainly have helped to take his mind off the crumbling *Violencia,* but his mind was off it anyway. And he had gone a bit sour on musicals in general. He called Mandarin back and told him he had changed his mind. Then he booked a private cottage on a small Caribbean island for "Mr. Paul Gurney and Guest."

After he and Angela had lounged in the sun for a few days, Gurney, having no idea in advance he was going to do this, began to create a long verse play, in heroic couplets, inspired by some of his experiences on *Violencia.* He felt it had some spirit to it, and he enjoyed seeing the pages pile up. On the days that it rained, Angela sat inside the cottage and helped Gurney, taking notes and then typing them on an old Underwood, supplied by the management. At other times, she roamed the island on a motorbike, holding on for dear life with that lovely one arm of hers.

When the work bogged down and Angela was out on the road, Gurney took strolls along the beach, making friends with a handsome, elderly British colonial type, who walked with a knotted cane and said he had once written with F. Scott Fitzgerald.

"What do you mean?" asked Gurney.

"I should think it would be perfectly clear," said the fellow. "We wrote together."

Gurney, who still did not understand how two people could write together, kept after the old gentleman.

"I'm afraid I don't follow you."

"Then bugger off," said the fellow with a certain colonial irritability. But when he himself tried to march off, he fell over in the sand and Gurney had to help him to his feet.

"Damned hip," said the fellow. "Went to war in '14 and it's never been the same. Trouble is, I like to take walks, do things, but I can't and it's a bloody shame."

"I think you're very courageous."

"Courageous my neck," said fellow. "It's just a bloody nuisance, that's all."

Gurney seemed to be saying all the wrong things to the elderly gentleman, and continued to compound his mistake.

"You're bloody well right, sir," he said, agreeably.

The fellow glared at him for making this remark, feeling *he* had exclusive rights to the "bloodies"—but somehow they became friendly all the same. He complimented Gurney on his lean, fit detective's body and said he had not overlooked the exquisite shape of "your lovely traveling companion."

"Yes," said Gurney, playing down the compliment, "she's quite a gal."

They saw each other every day along the beach and Gurney felt confident they would be getting together for lunches once they got back to the city. He seemed to require an older man for a friend. Now, of course, Gurney could no longer count on Clement Hartog to fill that role.

He thought often of the great director, picturing him back at Holliman, still trying to get the show in shape so that he could bring it to Broadway. He saw Hartog as a kind of theatrical Ahab, standing alone astride the battered deck of the sinking show, trying to keep it afloat, all the while combing the horizon with one demoniacal eye for a sign of that great white rave review. Gurney considered going back to help him, making another dramatic last-ditch appearance, and once again being saluted by the now tattered cast. And then he awakened in the middle of the night with a terrible fear that the show had opened on Broadway without him, and was an enormous smash, playing to packed houses. Single-handedly, battered and corpselike, with the life spilling out of him, Clement Hartog, in the greatest testimonial ever to the human spirit, had pumped life into the bleeding carcass of the dying animal of a show and miraculously turned it into a runaway hit. Or perhaps he had gotten help, and at that very moment another young, unknown librettist, who had put in only a week's work on the show, was sitting at Sardi's, wearing a cloak, smoking Russian cigarettes, and tossing off epigrams to network interviewers who hung on his every word.

Careful not to wake his companion, Gurney got out of bed, jumped on Angela's motorbike, and started off across the island to look for a newspaper. The stores, of course, had long been closed; perhaps he'd known that when he started out, and just wanted to get the feeling of a windswept drive around hairpin curves in the moonlight.

But his fear was genuine. When he got back from his ride, he was unable to sleep and remained on the cottage porch until dawn. Then he knocked on the door of the testy old colonial. The fellow hobbled forward, wearing a Dickensian nightgown of rich but conservatively chosen fabric. He admitted Gurney, who apologized for the intrusion.

"I was hoping, sir, that I might look through your *New York Times*. You mentioned having them sent to you each day."

The elderly fellow seemed, perhaps out of some sturdy sense of empire, to understand emergencies. He led Gurney to a stack of newspapers that were piled high on a bridge table. Holding his breath, Gurney raced through the theatrical sections of half a dozen of them until finally, with an enormous sense of relief, he came across the item he'd been hoping for.

MUSICAL SHUTS DOWN

The producers of *Violencia*, yielding to the generally poor out-of-town notices, have decided to close the show in Holliman after twenty-eight performances.

"Thank God," said Gurney.

"Some holding of yours take off?" asked the old fellow.

"No," said Gurney. "I don't fool around with the market. Just a little project that worked out."

The old man sat down in an armchair, lit his pipe, and seemed to be settling in for some amiably craggy early-morning chitchat. But Gurney merely thanked him for being so tolerant and walked out to the beach. He thought about the show, particularly that critical meeting at which Undertag, Toileau, and especially Hartog, with a silent plea in his eyes, had all looked over at Gurney for a sign of some fight, some fire in his belly—and he had been unable to help them.

There was no question he had let Hartog down badly. Perhaps if he had rolled up his sleeves and dug in during the last stage, the two of them might have brought it off after all. It occurred to him that perhaps all achievement that really mattered was tested by adversity. Were the participants worthy of the potential rewards? No doubt Catullus had pondered the question. He hadn't actually read Catullus, but Catullus was certainly on his list.

What was clear to Gurney was that he had failed to come up to the challenge.

Or maybe his future all along had been in heroic couplets.

Bad person or not, he felt a certain lightness as he raced off to tell Angela the news. He knew she would be good-natured about the early morning wake-up, though she'd look a little puzzled for a moment. But she would be entirely cheerful, as if it were perfectly reasonable to start the day a couple of hours earlier every once in a while. He loved that quality of hers. She certainly was easy on the nerves. He would really get to enjoy her now, probably for the first time—now that the show he had loved working on in Philip Undertag's office, adored in Winslow, and come to hate in Holliman, had had the last nail pounded into its brave and zesty little coffin.

Postscript

Telegram received by Paul Gurney, several months later.

Dear Paul,

      Caught closing performance of *Violencia* in Holliman. Most anxious to purchase film rights. If available, please have your representatives contact me as soon as possible.

      With every good wish,

      Hunt Feur,

      President, Bauhaus Productions

      P.S Am sending small Henry Moore sculpture as gesture of esteem.